Lost & Found

King Hill

First paperback edition: August 2025

Manufactured in the United States of America

Book cover, design, and editing
by Book Puma Author Services
BookPumaEdit.com

Cover photo by Oleg Purkhach
Cover photo model: Zhanna Logvenenko

ISBN: 979-8-218-73802-0

Dedication

This novel is dedicated to all those wonderful souls in this world who daily give love and kindness freely and who understand and celebrate the magic in living a life of awareness.

And to my loving wife, Dianne, who is the living example of love and kindness, and who, indeed, understands and finds the magic of life.

Contents

Endorsements

*"**LOVE IT!!!** Great adventure for all ages. This story is full of fun, excitement, twists and turns, and great characters."*

Carla Summers, middle school counselor

*"My daughter loves it. I love it. We are both hooked on Mariah and Emma, along with Bella and Sasha. **We couldn't put it down** and wanted to keep reading until the end."*

Barbara Teisdale, parent and homeschooler

*"**What an adventure!** What fun characters! What a great story!"*

Constance Cummings, realtor and podcaster

Acknowledgements

The author wishes to thank the following individuals whose insightful guidance, suggestions, assistance, and encouragement made this book possible:

- Kind House Ukraine Bakery and its founder and director, Glenda Moore, whose love, kindness, and inspiration were the basis of this novel and the character of Emma McCurdy.
- Zhanna Logvenenko, the beautiful adopted daughter of Glenda Moore, who graciously allowed her photo to be used on the cover of this novel. Her bravery and beauty well reflect that of her Ukrainian people and their incredible spirit to preserve their own identities, culture, and country.
- Jessica Hoskins, whose insights and assistance proved invaluable. She is also the basis for one of this novel's fictional characters, Jessica Kendred.
- Barbara Bowman, actress and friend whose constant support and encouragement made all the difference. And to her charming

dog and companion, Bella, on whom the character of Bella in the novel was based.

- Book Puma Author Services and the incomparable Amber Guffey.
- Rick Treon, book publisher and motion picture actor.
- My late father, artist and sculptor Jack King Hill, who possessed remarkable psychic abilities that he shared and encouraged with me, his son.

*I once was lost but now I'm found,
was blind but now I see.*

John Newton, *AMAZING GRACE*

1

She had no name, really. Only the one given to her by her first foster home, where she had lived after she was abandoned as a baby at the police station. Priscilla, sometimes to her disgust, was referred to as Prissy, and Prissy was not who she was. She didn't know what her real name was, or if she even had one, but she knew in her heart she was not a Priscilla. She knew she was not a Prissy. She hated both names, just like she hated the world where she had been placed.

Oh, the various foster parents and social workers were nice enough, she supposed. But they were just what she and some of the other children called "do-gooders." They meant well with their routines, guidelines, and unexplained religious doctrines, but it all seemed somewhat phony and more like a formula. This life she was living did not seem real, although it was all she had ever known. She was living a life shaped for her by people who did not know, understand, or see what she felt inside.

She knew early on she would leave this latest foster home in a series of temporary homes. It had been a hodgepodge of individual worlds and circumstances that forced her to assimilate, this time into the well-meaning but strict home of Herman and Carol Campbell.

She had no relatives. The few friends she had—adults and other children in care—were short-lived. They had their own paths to find. She knew this was not her path, not her home, not her people. She was determined to strike out on her own, to find people who could understand her. As scary as it was to consider an uncertain future, it was all she could think about night and day, hour after hour.

When the annual Foster Families Halloween Carnival rolled around, she dressed in a gypsy costume, disguised her backpack with a large shawl, and disappeared into the shadows as the crowd swirled around her like falling leaves. She was gone, and it wasn't until much later that night that anyone noticed.

She took the fresh start as an opportunity to find the right name. She chose Mariah after an older girl at another foster home. That Mariah was fiercely independent and smart, reading her books, writing in her journal, and keeping company only with her aging cat.

That Mariah loved listening to music. Whenever Priscilla was allowed to visit her, she would play song after song of modern pop, rap, techno, folk tunes, and even movie soundtracks. That Mariah softly confided to Priscilla that she had been named after a song—*They Call the Wind Moriah*—by her grandmother, who had raised the girl until she died.

That Mariah seemed wild and carefree, like a gypsy. Priscilla admired her and her defiant love of freedom in the highly restricted world of foster care. That Mariah dressed in colorful clothes and scarves that would have been at home in the 1960s hippie culture.

No more Priscilla. From now on, as she shuffled from alley to alley, camping out in empty warehouses and trash dumpsters, she would be Mariah. It wasn't much, she told herself, but it was a beginning.

At least she had a name that fit. It was soft, but also grown. It had its own history, plus a new history she would create. It seemed a good name for a survivor, and that was what she had become. Mariah survived by gathering food from restaurant trash bins and earning a few dollars here and there by doing small chores for some elderly folks on the ragged side of town.

No one ever found her, though the authorities searched. Mariah was too clever, and she stayed away from the places where she expected they would check.

One day after a while on the streets, Mariah caught a ride to Brewster from a truck driver, telling him she was going to live with her grandmother who didn't own or drive a car. Once there, she felt confident that no one would be searching for her. She survived as the new Mariah always had, finding her way in the shadows.

A noise woke her from her sleep one night, but it was more than a noise. It was as if somebody—or something—was calling out, lonely and scared. She unwrapped herself from the newspaper, pushed aside the remnants of a leftover Big Mac she had scrounged, and climbed out of the dumpster. Mariah shone her flashlight on a pile of cardboard placed among the restaurant's trash containers. It was then that Mariah saw—or really, felt—the presence of the scrawny, frightened dog. The dog shivered, but did not seem dangerous.

Mariah looked into the dog's eyes, and the dog raised its head and looked back into hers. Both knew things were okay. Instantly, it was clear to them that one would care for the other. It was clear that they needed each other.

Mariah approached the dog slowly, wrapped her shawl around the dog, and cradled it like a child. From that moment, they would be inseparable.

"What is your name?" Mariah asked sweetly, as if the dog could talk.

Staring into Mariah's eyes, the dog seemed to understand. And without speaking, the dog answered. "Bella. My name is Bella."

Mariah could hear the words, though the dog made no sound at all. Holding up the dog to face her, Mariah repeated the name as a question. "Bella?"

The dog smiled and licked her face. The silent communication was immediate and direct. "Yes, Bella. And who are you?"

"I call myself Mariah. I will take care of you,

Bella. I promise."

As the final words came out of Mariah's mouth, her new friend fell asleep softly in her arms.

It was frigid that night. Mariah and her new friend snuggled tightly against each other back in the dumpster, wrapped in the shawl and a small children's blanket she had taken from her last foster home.

At dawn, their eyes popped open. The scent of cinnamon rolls and other baked goods wafted their way from farther down the alley. Warmth, goodness, and even safety somehow seemed to travel along with the aromas.

Mariah lifted Bella out of the dumpster and placed her on the ground, then shouldered her backpack. "Bella girl, I think we should follow our nose. Well, make that noses."

They ran toward the source of the treats. The sun was just coming up as the two approached the back of what must be a bakery or café. It turned out to be both. And it turned out to be a much-needed miracle for Bella and Mariah.

The shop's back door burst open as they stood still, taking in the delightful scents of spices and bread. Out came an older woman, who seemed round from top to bottom, carrying a sack of trash. The woman spotted the two travelers as she turned toward the trash can against the wall.

She smiled at them. "Well, what and who do we have here?"

Mariah and Bella were silent, with the dog hovered close to Mariah's leg. After a second or two, they backed up several feet, adding distance between them and the woman.

The woman smiled again. This time, it was the sincerest smile Mariah had ever seen.

The older woman did not move when she spoke again. "It's okay. Don't be afraid. I won't hurt either of you. All God's creatures are welcome here. I am Emma Gail McCurdy, and I run this bakery. Please, won't you come inside? It's very cold out here, and it's warm by the oven. I bet you're both hungry, and I know just the thing to warm you up."

The woman motioned toward the door, then stretched out both of her hands in welcome. Mariah hesitantly walked toward her as Bella followed slowly, stuck to Mariah's side.

"You are welcome here, and so is your doggie," Emma assured. "I told you my name. May I know yours?"

For some reason, Mariah was no longer afraid. The older woman seemed nice and safe, so she gave a shy smile in return. "My name is Mariah, and this is Bella."

"Well, welcome, Mariah. Welcome, Bella. Welcome to Aunt Emma's Kind House Bakery." Emma held the screen door open and beckoned the duo closer.

Inside, it was magical. Mariah knew instantly that she and Bella were safe with this woman. The bakery was warm, really warm, thanks to the ovens, stove, and a small heater in the corner.

And the smells. Oh, the smells! Sweet, savory, and that overwhelming feeling of being surrounded by light and warmth and goodness.

Yes, Mariah told herself, *that's the word: Goodness.* Mariah's head spun as she took it all in—red and yellow curtains over the sparkling windows, row upon row of fresh baked goods stacked on the racks of wheeled carts.

"Here. Mariah, you can sit here," Emma said, then motioned to a high-backed stool near a small table at one end of the room.

"And Bella," she said as she smiled at the dog, "you can rest here on this."

As Emma folded and placed a blanket near Mariah's feet, Bella looked up into the woman's eyes and her warm, comforting smile. Bella knew then that they were in good hands, so she settled into the blanket.

Mariah glanced down at Bella, who told Mariah in her own way that they were okay. "We are safe now," Bella said without words. "This is good, and this woman is good."

"Yes, she is," Mariah replied aloud.

"What was that? What were you saying?" Emma turned back toward her guests.

"Oh, nothing," Mariah said. "I was just telling Bella she was right. We are safe, and you are nice."

"Is that what Bella told you?" Emma asked. "You know, dogs can indeed talk. All animals can. The only problem is humans don't listen. They just want to do all the talking."

Bella looked at Emma and then back at Mariah. "She is right, you know. I like this lady. Oh, Mariah, can we stay here?" Bella pleaded with her eyes and a soft whimper.

Emma watched the interaction, then nodded at Mariah. "Of course you can. You can stay as long as you like. Now, let's get you both something to eat."

And she did. Emma prepared scrambled eggs with cheese and bits of bacon, along with the yummiest warm toast slathered with a blanket of orange marmalade. She placed it before Mariah with a large glass of milk. The woman then laid a plate of sausage pieces and scrambled eggs and a bowl of fresh water down beside Bella.

As the two eagerly ate, Emma hummed a melody both lively and mysterious. Mariah devoured the meal. Before she could ask what the tune was, Emma had filled her plate again.

"Yes, I know you're hungry, both of you. Oh, and the tune you are wondering about is an old Irish ditty that my late husband, Mr. McCurdy, would sing to me. Michael was his name, and *Molly Malone* is the song."

Emma moved about the kitchen with a speed and deliberateness that Mariah couldn't believe someone of her age could manage. The woman stirred a pot here, removed a tray from an oven there, placed finished items on display racks, and never once stopped.

After a while, Emma noticed Mariah and Bella nodding their heads sleepily after eating all that was placed before them. "Ah, I see the sandman is calling," Emma sang out like a melody. "Well then, come with me, loves, and we'll find a place for you to rest."

Mariah and Bella followed Emma through a side door and down a small hallway into a medium-sized room with a bed, a small table, a lamp, a dresser, a closet, and an open door revealing a bathroom.

"Come in, come in. I don't use this anymore. I live upstairs in my apartment. Here, you both can rest. I have to hurry and get ready to open the bakery soon, so get some sleep and we'll talk later. And don't worry: you'll be safe."

Emma pointed to a second door. "That opens to small garden and the alley. If Bella needs to go out, you can use it. Or, if you decide to leave, it's your path to do so. But, girls, I think we may become friends and help each other."

"You have been very kind, Mrs. umm?"

"Just call me Emma." The woman smiled

warmly in response.

"But I don't have much money," Mariah said sadly. "I mean to pay you for the food."

"Keep your money, and consider it a gift. A kindness. That's part of the name of this bakery, by the way. I named it the Kind House Bakery, and kindness is as important here as money. Now, rest. We can talk later. I must get back to preparing for my customers."

Before closing the door from the hall, Emma gazed back at the two guests, who were already fast asleep. It was a picture in time. A captured moment like a photograph of a young girl with dark, flowing tangled hair and crumpled dirty clothes cradling a small dog in her arms. It was the beginning of a new day, a new adventure, and a new friendship for them all.

2

All good things come in threes, it has been said. The three wise men. The Father, the Son, and Holy Spirit. The three little pigs. Three meals a day: breakfast, lunch, and dinner. Three wishes gifted by Aladdin's genie. Yes, magic often happens in threes. And the same seemed to apply to Mariah, Bella, and her newfound friendship with the kind woman named Emma.

This morning, like the past three mornings, came early. Mariah was up, dressed, and eager to help Emma prepare the bakery for customers. Mariah loved being there. She loved the smells, the pots and pans, the washing, the baking and . . . well, all of it.

But most of all, she had come to love Emma and her kindness. After the morning rush, Emma sat in her high-backed chair in the corner of the kitchen as Mariah arranged the leftover baked goods and tidied up.

"Come here, Mariah. Pull up your stool beside me." Emma wore a solemn look.

Nervous, Mariah glanced over by the door to where Bella lay on her blanket. The dog raised her head, telling Mariah with her big brown eyes that she was nervous, too.

Emma gave a warm smile to ward off their unease. "It is time to grasp the nettle, as my late husband Mr. McCurdy would say when coming to terms with a serious situation. He wasn't one to put off facing decisions, and neither am I. You and Bella have been here for three days now, and I must confess that you have become a special part of this bakery in those three days. And, more importantly, you've become a special person to me. I have no children, no living relatives aside from my younger sister who lives back east and is . . . well, let's just say that Constance is not a people person. But back to you. We have a decision to make, you and I, and, of course, Bella."

Mariah squeezed her hands together tightly, fearing what would come next. She sat rigidly and stared down at her hands rather than meet

Emma's eyes.

Emma rose from her chair slowly and paced the room as she continued. "I don't know you, really, aside from what you confided in me about being in foster homes and running away. I can tell you are sweet, hardworking, sincere, and honest. Honesty is the most important part. We must be honest. I am sure the people with the foster home and the whole foster system are worried sick, wondering about your whereabouts and contacting the authorities. I want to help you, and I certainly want to do the right thing. So, let me put it to you directly."

Emma paused in front of Mariah, taking her chin in her hands and raising Mariah's head so could see her eyes. "Mariah."

No response.

"Mariah," she repeated. "Would you like to stay here with me at the bakery a little longer? Would you like—"

Mariah jumped to her feet and clung tightly to Emma. "Yes! Yes! Yes! I'd like to stay here longer. I'd like to stay here *forever*."

Emma smiled widely as Bella joined in the embrace, barking and leaping around the two.

"Well, forever is a long time, so let's just take it a step at a time," Emma said. "The first step will be to contact those foster parents and all involved immediately to let them know you are safe. Then, of course, will come the questions, the meetings, the interviews, and all the rest of the legal mumbo jumbo. But I promise you this: I will be forthright and provide all the information and such needed for you to stay here with me, God willing. And as Mr. McCurdy would say, I have a feeling God is willing. He seemed to take a liking to the Irish, to the kind and to the well-meaning, and I think you and I may qualify. May the saints be blessed, Mariah, and welcome to what is hopefully your new home."

"Oh, Emma, yes please. I trust you and well, I guess, love you. I want to stay. Please, please don't let them take me away. Please," Mariah pleaded as she hugged Emma.

"Now, now, dear. Don't let a worry enter your head. I make a good living here. I am well-known and well, truth be told, respected. And, dear one, I am not without my own little army, shall we say. I have friends and customers that are lawyers, judges, city officials, church folk, and the like, and I think they'll all be coming to our aid. I am thinking it's going to be mostly forms and formalities. It will take some time, though, that's for sure. Nothing with the government happen fast. But happen, it will."

Taking a pen and notepad from a nearby table, Emma motioned for Mariah to sit beside her. "Now, about grasping that nettle. I need your confidence, your cooperation, your help so I can help you, and, most of all, I need your honesty. Let's start at the beginning. I have a feeling Mariah may not be your real name, so let's begin there."

Mariah told her everything. She talked without hesitation or fear. Mariah told Emma about being Priscilla, about being abandoned, about bouncing between several foster homes, and about her final placement this last year with the Campbells.

Mariah calmly explained she left because she didn't feel like she belonged, because she hated the mechanical nature of her daily routine and chores. The foster parents, though nice, only seemed interested in her behaving and "growing in the Lord," as they called it. Finally, through tears, Mariah told Emma she couldn't have pets, couldn't have close friends, and couldn't spend time with others her age unless it was at school or at highly supervised church activities.

As the oldest in the home, Mariah had been relegated to supervising and caring for the younger house members—two boys about six years old and a girl about seven who constantly wore Mariah's clothes, lied, and seemed to be the Campbells' favorite.

"Wasn't there anyone to check on you?" Emma asked. "Maybe a caseworker or someone to make sure you were doing well?"

"Kind of," Mariah replied. "The caseworker seems nice, but she only came once or twice a month, and then just asked a couple of questions, filled out some papers, and repeatedly nodded as I tried to explain my feelings. All Miss Martin would say was, 'That's nice. You're lucky to have the Campbells as your foster parents.'"

Mariah wrote down the Campbells' cellphone numbers and home address, as well as Miss Martin's full name, Beverly Martin.

Emma reviewed it dutifully, then placed the paper under a heavy glass paperweight on her desk. "Well, today's Friday," she said as she rose from her seat. "I will call tonight before we turn in. My guess is that they will come here tomorrow. But today, you must meet the rest of the family."

Mariah stepped back in surprise. "I thought you lived here by yourself. I didn't know other people lived here."

Emma gave a deep laugh that made her dress and apron billow out like the wind filling an old ship's sails. "Other people? Land's sake, no child. By others, I meant creatures, living friends. You have seen and collected eggs from the chickens we keep in the large coop, but you need to know them individually and their personalities. And believe me, they are distinct personalities. Come, let's go greet them formally and tell them that you are now a part of our little family."

Taking Mariah by the hand, Emma led her outside through a side door. Bella circled her blanket and rested after the excitement of Emma's invitation.

Emma stooped down, entered the coop, then brought out a chicken to hand to Mariah. "Okay, here we go. First off is Callie. She is happy-go-lucky and always produces good eggs without hesitation."

"She's very fluffy," Mariah said, "and I like her

color."

Emma returned Callie and brought forth the next. "This is Henreitta, the oldest and the quietest. She is not fussy, just dependable."

The process was repeated. "Next, we have Delores. She's named after a friend because her eyes sparkle with mischievousness, just like my friend. Hold her up and look into her eyes."

Mariah smiled, and Delores seemed to smile back before Emma picked her up again.

"Now, here is Jenny. Hold her tight, or she'll jump out of your arms and make a run for it. She likes it here, she told me once, but she also likes adventure. I think maybe you two might have something in common."

Mariah and Emma laughed loudly together, and they just couldn't stop. The girl sensed that even Jenny enjoyed the joke, as she quit struggling. Jenny turned her head to Mariah, somehow smiling knowingly.

"Yes, just what I thought," Emma said, watching the two. "Jenny knows an accomplice when she sees one. Now then, neither of you two get any wild ideas, okay?"

"Okay," Mariah agreed with a laugh as Jenny went back into the coop.

"Here is Suzanna. I think she's Jewish because she only seems to like certain feed, different from the others, so maybe that feed is kosher. Who knows? Suzanna never lays eggs on Saturdays—the Jewish Sabbath—so that's another reason. She is sweet and mild as a kitten, and the others seem to like her."

"And last but certainly not least," Emma said with a tone like a trumpet fanfare when she returned again from the coop, "is Pooka the Great, or the Great Pooka."

Pooka was the largest chicken Mariah had ever seen. The beautiful, golden-feathered bird held her head high like a queen. As Mariah reached out to touch Pooka, the chicken recoiled and gave her a dismissive, defiant look.

"Oh, don't mind Pooka, dear," Emma assured her. "She just informed me she needs more time to get to know you and to make up her own mind on whether you are worthy of her attention."

"She's beautiful!" Mariah exclaimed.

Pooka turned toward Mariah, raised her head regally, and then lifted one leg as if in agreement.

"Yes," Emma said. "She knows it, too. I think she would like it if you said she was M-A-G-N-I-F-I-C-E-N-T. . . . Pooka's smart for sure, but she doesn't spell. So, now say the word and watch her reaction."

"Pooka is magnificent," Mariah announced.

Slowly but surely, Pooka the Great puffed out her chest and flew the short distance into Mariah's arms.

"Well then, that seemed to do the trick," Emma said. "Chickens, like all great creatures, can talk, listen, and feel emotions. It's just that most humans are too busy, too proud, or too ignorant to learn that. Congratulations! They all seem to like you."

"I like them, too," Mariah said proudly. She gave a cute little curtsy toward the chickens in the coop, then she and Emma giggled.

"Now, I think it's time for you and Bella to meet the last member of our group. This special one has powers and sensibilities beyond most creatures."

"What is it?" Mariah asked. "What kind of animal is it?"

"Oh, you'll see soon enough," Emma said as she ushered Mariah back inside the home.

Bella rose and stretched, then looked curiously at them.

"Follow me, both of you," Emma said as she led them down a long hallway and then up a flight of stairs.

She opening the door to a surprisingly large room. "This is the apartment, my living quarters, where my Michael and I lived as we developed our enterprises. It encompasses the whole top floor. Come, I'll show you around."

Mariah followed with a hint of fear, and Bella stuck close to her leg.

Sensing their hesitation, Emma leaned down to pet Bella and to assure her with a soft word that she was welcome here. In the first room, large windows across two sides were fitted with beautiful heavy drapes that could shut out the bright exterior lights when needed. Large chairs and two older couches covered in rich hues of taupe and turquoise added a sense of comfort to the room. Throw pillows and folded blankets adorned each. Large round or horizontal rugs warmed the room's glistening wood floors.

Accent tables held photos, cards, letters, and porcelain figurines.

"You're welcome to take a closer look at anything you'd like," Emma told Mariah. "These are items my husband and I collected through the years, along with others that were gifts. We . . . I mean, I cherish each one."

Bella's ears stood up sharply after a sudden sound. She rose to rigid attention and eyed a blanket on the couch nearest the eastern window. She started barking, but Emma just laughed.

"Relax, Bella," she said. "Come on out, Sasha."

The most beautiful, pure white cat emerged from its warm cocoon of a blanket and nuzzled her head against Emma's hand. Mariah was spellbound by the cat's beauty, especially her spectacular sapphire blue eyes that seemed to radiate both intelligence and beauty.

The cat leaped from the couch into the girl's arms and looked up at her. Mariah was surprised, but not as much as Bella. Bella stood up on hind legs and tried to reach Sasha with her paws.

Emma didn't miss a beat, taking Sasha from Mariah's arms and placing her on the floor right in front of the dog. Bella froze.

"It's okay," Emma said. "You're okay. Sasha won't hurt you. Unlike some cats, Sasha isn't afraid or aggressive toward other animals or people. Sasha, please welcome Bella to our home."

Carefully and cautiously, she approached Bella, who started to growl. Sasha didn't back away. Instead, she slowly leaned into Bella and licked her muzzle. After the shock wore off, the dog relaxed somewhat and circled Sasha. The cat stood perfectly still as Bella sniffed her. When she was done, Bella stopped.

The animals stood frozen like statues for what seemed the longest time until Bella finally walked to Sasha and licked the cat's fur again and again. Sasha softly nuzzled against Bella, then both leaped onto a couch and lay down next to each other.

"Well, that didn't take long," Emma said. "I see our Sasha and Bella are best friends, as it should be. Let's leave these two to get acquainted while I show you the rest of the apartment."

Mariah followed with a nod.

"Here is the bathroom, and yes, it's ridiculously large," Emma said. "Look at the huge antique tub on claw feet. The brass fixtures came from France. It holds gallons and gallons of water, and is perfect for a warm soaking bath after a full day. The water bill gets large, but I'll let you in on a secret."

She leaned down and whispered into Mariah's ear. "I have money, dear, lots and lots of it. Not to brag, but my dearest husband left me well taken care of, and, of course, we both worked for years. We added to his inheritance with money of our own. No one here—not me, not you, not the animals—will ever have to worry. First Federal Bank and Trust knows I'm one of their biggest and best customers, and they are keen to wisely help oversee and manage this estate. As you will soon know, this complex has many different spaces and venues. It is much more than the bakery and small downstairs apartment that is now your and Bella's room. No, there is much more. Next is the kitchen, down this hall."

The kitchen was like something out of an Old World European photograph. It had a brick floor, a fireplace, modern appliances, and windows with bright gypsy curtains. Glass beads and colored bottles filtered the light, and a large table with four chairs stood in the center of the room. Brass and steel pots and pans of every shape and size hung on racks suspended from the ceiling. The countertops were a maple granite, and the wooden pantry and kitchen cabinets were honey-colored and pristine.

Mariah marveled at each feature. "How warm! How lovely, and how very inviting."

"Yes, it is, dear. It's a great way to greet the day every morning with a cup of tea and spoonful of honey. But come, there's more to see."

Mariah followed her to room after room. There was a sewing room, a laundry room, a dining room, a sitting room, and then Emma's bedroom. Her sanctuary had a large, canopied bed, nightstands, a chest of drawers, chairs and lamps, a huge walk-in closet and a full-length antique mirror next to a beautifully carved oversized dressing table.

And with a flourish, Emma opened the door to the largest room of the living quarters. Mariah felt like she was entering a magic portal into another world, another dimension, another reality.

Emma saw her expression and beamed. "Yes! I knew you would like it, and hopefully you'll grow to cherish it as I do. It's my favorite room in the house. It is our library, study, and room of reflection. Michael and I would often eat dinner here by candlelight or relax by the fireplace."

Emma walked toward the large stone fireplace with a majestic wood mantel. She touched the stones that had been carefully placed to form the hearth and chimney. To the left and right, each wall was covered with floor-to-ceiling bookcases holding all sorts of books. Then, there was the art: paintings illuminated by soft accent lights. Aside from the table in the center, there were chairs and small tables, nooks, and even window seats with cushions to curl up on. The room had the feel of an old ship's cabin or a log cabin in the forest.

"It is the best room in the whole world," Mariah whispered.

"I think so too, dear. I knew you would understand," Emma said. "Let me show you a special feature. I love music. Michael knew music like no one else, and he taught me about all different styles from classical to jazz, American folk to Russian folk tunes, rock, and even the blues. You name it, and he knew it. Many, many nights were spent here, far from the maddening crowd, as the old saying goes, just sharing special moments between us. He loved the singer Joni Mitchell and told me once that the lyrics of one of her songs seemed to sum up the whole mystical experience of being transported to another place and time while embracing special music in a special place like this. The words were, 'Love is touching souls.' He was right, you know. Find out for yourself. There is the wall of old vinyl records and CDs, and even some cassette tapes."

Mariah looked confused, which made Emma laugh. "Go pick one out, and I'll show you how to play it."

Mariah scanned the shelves and titles, but still seemed at a loss.

"Here, try this," Emma said, handing her the cover of an old record, the soundtrack to the movie *Cabaret*. Mariah plopped down on a soft ottoman as Emma placed the record on a turntable and turned up the volume.

The world stopped. Mariah was transported to a new place, this new, wonderful world that would be her home. Her incredible, mystical, magical home.

3

The morning sun was bright and full of promise as Emma woke Mariah with a soft pat on the back. Mariah yawned, then startled awake.

"Oh no, I'm late!" Mariah said as she jumped out of bed. "You're late. What time is it? We should already be at the bakery. I'll get cleaned up and dressed quickly."

"Relax." Emma smiled at her as she gently spoke. "Today is Saturday, and I have arranged for my friend and bakery volunteer Helen and her cousin, Samantha, to run the bakery. She knows all the ropes and what to do. This is our day to celebrate the weekend. Now, get dressed, and I'll meet you at the foot of the stairs."

Mariah stifled another small yawn as Bella stretched her hind legs and wagged her tail excitedly. They arrived at the stairs just in time to watch Emma descend in a colorful print dress.

"Bella girl, you will have to stay here," Emma explained. "We'll be back soon, and I'll make you a big breakfast and lunch."

She took Mariah by the hand. "Let's take the shortcut through this hallway."

"Shortcut to what?" Mariah asked.

"To another of my businesses and another extended group of our little family."

Curiosity carried Mariah through one door then another until she and Emma entered a small-but-bustling kitchen. The smells and music were both inviting. A short, overweight man with a huge mustache turned to greet them.

"Ah, buenos dias, Madre," he said with a bow to each. "Buenos dias, chica."

"And top of the morning to you, Mateo, my friend and brother," Emma replied. "This is Mariah, hopefully a new addition to our family. She came to us a few days ago and already has shown a great spirit and willingness to learn."

"Indeed," Mateo nodded somewhat wisely. "Well, well, please come into the dining room and I will prepare you a special desayuno."

Mariah, puzzled by the foreign word, looked

to Emma.

"That's breakfast, dear, in Spanish. Mateo is renowned for dishes, both the everyday and the specialties of his native Mexico."

After directing them to a table by the front window, Mateo pulled out the chair for Emma first, then Mariah, as he seated them formally. His lips pursed to let out a short whistle, and a young twentysomething woman in a simple-but-stylish skirt and blouse seemed to appear out of thin air.

"This," Mateo said with a flourish, "is my wonderful daughter, Veronica. She and my wife, Delores, help me run this wonderful Café de Esperanza."

Veronica smiled warmly and stood next to her father as he continued.

"Delores is in the kitchen, cooking as usual. Veronica, bring the young girl orange juice and Madre Emma her coffee with cream. Apurate!"

"Yes, father." She set off, then returned within what seemed just seconds with the drinks.

Mateo, bowing once more, spoke again. "Excuse me, please. Together, Delores and I shall prepare a special breakfast for you. And I think I know just the thing."

He winked at Mariah. "Once again, welcome to Esperanza."

As their host disappeared into the kitchen, Mariah was again left confused. "What is esper . . . the word the man used?"

"Esperanza is the name of this café, and its motto," Emma said. "It means hope. And hope, along with great food, is what Mateo and his family serve here. Hope is dished out to people of all backgrounds and circumstances who come here. His name, Mateo, means gift of God, and he was truly a gift from God to Mr. McCurdy and me when we launched this restaurant. We needed a good manager, and he has been that gift ever since. You see, Mariah, there is truly magic in the world. Magic is all around us all the time. We just need to open our hearts and our minds to realize it. Names have magic and meaning as well."

After quietly taking in Emma's words, Mariah had a question. "Wow! How do you know all these things?"

"Well, dear, I was an English teacher and college

professor for many years, but my husband was also wise. We read a great deal, and we traveled. Those travels took us to different cultures and places where we learned more. Part of that was about powerful names."

"What does your name mean?" she asked Emma with a slight tilt of her head.

Emma looked across the table. "Well, it means something like universal or whole. In my case, I think it means that I seek to make things whole, to surround myself with love, and to make things that are incomplete, or even broken, whole again. Like in baking, you take all manner of different ingredients and you make a whole tasty treat with care and skill."

Emma laughed gently. "Now, what's interesting is *your* name. Not so much the name you were assigned or given, but the name you chose for yourself. Mariah means wise, and you are indeed wise beyond your years, dear one. I have watched as you take in everything around you— sights and sounds, smells, and even people and animals. You have gifts, and I think you can and will use them wisely."

Mateo and Veronica suddenly appeared carrying trays and placed breakfast plates before their guests. For Emma, there were scrambled eggs, bacon, and warm toast with butter. For Mariah, there was a large plate of golden pancakes stacked high with fresh strawberries and whipped cream, her choice of blueberry or maple syrup, eggs, bacon, and even a glass of milk.

Mariah's eyes widened. "I have never, ever, ever seen such a breakfast. Wow! Thank you. Thank you."

"Enjoy!" Veronica said as she and Mateo retreated to the kitchen.

After a simple prayer of thanks, Emma encouraged Mariah to eat. And eat she did. They ate without talking really, just smiling in between bites and nodding at the bounty of goodness placed before them.

"This was the best breakfast—or anything—I have ever had in my life," Mariah said once she had her fill. "Thank you. Thank you."

"You are welcome," Emma said with a smile. "To paraphrase a saying by one of my favorite characters in one of my favorite books, 'Life is a banquet, and most poor suckers are starving to death.'"

Mariah's eyes showed her confusion.

"I'm sure you have heard the expression that people need to slow down and smell the roses," Emma continued. "Well, I agree. To me and the late Mr. McCurdy, life was meant to be an adventure, a magical experience to be embraced and enjoyed. Unfortunately, to most people, life is something to simply be endured. Thankfully, you and I are not like most people, are we?"

Emma winked, and Mariah giggled. "Oh, Emma, being with you is the best. Everything is new and wonderful and magical, and I don't want it to ever end."

"I don't either, dear, but I learned a long time ago that life offers the good and the not-so-good. We must make our own choices and then live with the outcomes. Today, Mariah, you have a decision to make, and it's not one to make lightly."

Mariah raised her eyebrows. "A decision? I don't understand."

"Let me explain," Emma said patiently. "Last night, I called your former foster home, explained you were safe with me, and gave my address and such. The woman who answered,

Mrs. Campbell, Carol Campbell, was beside herself. She was so relieved you were safe here. She explained that she and her husband would contact the caseworker and make plans for you to return. I told her that I wanted what was best for you and that I, well . . . I told her I wanted to speak to the officials to see . . ."

Mariah finished the sentence. "To see if I could stay here with you? Oh, Emma, can that happen? I mean, can you do that? Oh, please? Oh—"

Emma interrupted her. "Let's not be putting the cart before the horse. This morning, before I woke you, I got a call from a Mrs. Jessica Kendred with the Social Services Department. We set an appointment for her to come here and talk with us. Mrs. Kendred will make her assessment and discuss your future. She will be here shortly, around eleven this morning."

Mariah began to cry softly and quietly at first, then it gave way to sobbing that shook her shoulders.

Emma reached over and grabbed her hands. "Now, now, don't cry," she said. "No need for tears or fears till we hear her out, and, more importantly, till she hears us out."

She dabbed at Mariah's tears with her napkin. "Now, please give me a smile. This is our chance to make our case. Understand?"

"Yes," Mariah whispered, "but I just want to stay here with you and with Bella and Sasha and this world."

Mateo approached them as Emma stood up. "How was everything? Good, I hope."

"Very good, as usual. Thanks, Mateo."

"And you, little one, did you enjoy your breakfast?"

Mariah nodded her head. "Yes, yes. Thank you very much."

As the two guests left through the front door, Mariah heard Mateo speaking in Spanish.

"Vaya con Dios," he began. "Go with God."

Looking back over her shoulder, Mariah glanced up at the bold red letters painted on the café's sign: *CAFÉ ESPERANZA*. "Hope."

Yes, Mariah repeated to herself, *hope. That's what I want and what I need.*

Emma led the way to a storefront next door.

Its bright green sign, painted on an arch over the doorway, read *EMERALD ENTERPRISES*. Mariah enjoyed the four-leaf clover design under the words.

Taking a key from her purse, Emma unlocked the door and turned on the lights. Mariah followed her to the front office, where there was a large desk, lamps, tables, and a bookcase spanning one wall stacked high with ledgers and binders of all sizes. On the other walls hung paintings of landscapes and portraits of stern-looking men.

"What is this place?" Mariah asked quietly.

"It is my late husband's office. Well, I guess it's my office now. I come once or twice a week, sometimes more, to pay bills, complete payroll for our businesses, catch up on business mail, and such. It has been this way since the beginning, and I didn't change a thing after Mr. McCurdy passed."

Mariah took in the space and nodded. "Wow, you have more rooms and hallways. It's like, like a . . ."

Emma laughed. "A maze? Yes, I know."

She sat at her ancient, oversized rolltop desk,

then continued. "You're right. There are more twists and turns and surprises than the famous Kildare Maze shaped like Saint Brigid's Cross. Now, I'll impart an important piece of wisdom that Michael, bless his soul, was fond of saying: 'Life is like a maze. You have to go through different things to get where you want to be.'"

The unexpected ring of the doorbell sent Emma to her feet. When she opened the door, she gave a warm smile to the woman waiting there, who seemed to be about thirty and carried a satchel.

"Hello," the stranger said. "I'm Jessica Kendred from the state's Social Services Department." She stuck her out her hand to Emma. "You must be Mrs. McCurdy, the one who called me."

"Indeed, I am. One and the same. Welcome. Please, come in and have a seat. We'll go to the rest of the complex, where the bakery and living quarters and such are, but I wanted to meet here first in the event you needed financial data, background documents, or other materials."

"That's very kind of you." The woman smiled sympathetically. "All that will come in time, but first I want to get acquainted."

Mrs. Kendred turned to lay eyes on Mariah, who nervously crouched in a chair near the corner. The social worker gave a large, warm smile and rose to greet the girl. "Well, hello there. You must be Priscilla. I have heard so much about you. I am glad to finally meet you, and I look forward to us getting to know each other and becoming friends."

Mariah raised her head slowly. "My name is not Priscilla now," she said with a hint of defiance. "It's Mariah, and you're not the regular caseworker. That's Beverly."

Without hesitating, Jessica spoke again. "No, I'm not. I am Jessica, and I asked to work with you, Priscilla. . . . Oh, excuse me. Mariah."

After watching the exchange between the two play out, Emma smiled and gave a conspiratorial wink to Jessica.

"Well, Mariah, why don't we show Mrs. Kendred our way back through the café kitchen to the bakery, your room, and the rest? You lead the way," Emma said as she walked over to Mariah and brought her to her feet for a warm hug.

Jessica chuckled. "Why not? Sounds like a real

adventure."

It was a test, of sorts. Emma wanted to see just how rigid this social worker would be and how she thought and functioned. And as Jessica politely followed Mariah as the morning progressed, Emma decided she had passed with glowing marks.

Mariah led Jessica through the bakery, explaining every machine, procedure, and nuance as an adult would. She showed Jessica to her bedroom, then turned to take her through the hall and up the stairs to Emma's room.

"Before we do that," Jessica started, "would it be all right if I started the interview with just Mariah? And then afterwards, I will interview Mrs. McCurty alone."

Emma smiled. "Of course. Mariah will bring you up to the second floor and my quarters when you two are finished."

Mariah took in a quick breath. "Please stay here with me."

"You'll be fine, dear," Emma assured her. "Mrs. Kendred is right. You two need some privacy to talk and get to know each other. I'll see you later, and our guest can meet Sasha and Bella then."

Jessica turned to Mariah. "Sasha and Bella? Other children?"

"No, Mrs. Kendred," Mariah said with a boisterous laugh, and much of her initial tension evaporated. "Sasha is the most beautiful cat you have ever seen, and Bella . . . well, Bella is my doggie. She is smart and an orphan like me. But then . . . you wouldn't know about orphans, I guess, other than with your job, I mean."

Jessica gave a soft, genuine laugh. "Oh, but I would. I was an orphan, too."

"You? You were an orphan?"

"Yes, and please just call me Jessica. I want us to become friends. Let me help you, one orphan to another."

The morning and early afternoon passed quickly. Mariah's confidence and pride returned as Jessica listened and took notes. When it was Jessica's turn to ask the questions, Mariah answered honestly and without hesitation.

"Thank you for being so candid and honest," Jessica said as she finally closed her laptop.

Mariah looked deeply into Jessica's eyes. "Can I stay here? I mean, can I just stay here with

Emma and live here and not go back? Please, don't make me go back there."

Jessica walked over to sit down beside Mariah, who was perched on her bed, and then took her hand. "I have no intention whatsoever of sending you back," Jessica said with a smile. "I just have to make sure what is best for you."

"This is best for me. Please. Please," Mariah begged. "Just let me stay here."

"My job is to make sure you're safe, cared for, and happy," Jessica said. "From what I've seen thus far, that seems to be more than the case. Now, take me to Mrs. McCurdy. I need to talk with her."

Mariah complied and led the way. "And here are the famous Bella and Sasha," she said as they walked in.

Once Jessica extended her hand for Bella to sniff, the dog approached cautiously and made her appraisal. Once satisfied, Bella went to Mariah and gave a single bark.

Looking into her eyes, Bella assured her girl. "This is a good lady," the dog explained without words. "She can be trusted. She likes you. And she likes me, I can tell. She can be our friend, I think."

Mariah held Bella in her arms. "I think so, too," she replied without realizing she was talking aloud.

Jessica smiled without judgment. Sasha walked a tight circle around Jessica a couple of times, while the social worker remained still. The cat then sidled up next to her, rubbing her fur against Jessica's legs and purring soft approval.

Emma spoke next. "I think she likes you, Mrs. Kendred."

"Well, I certainly like her, too," Jessica said. "She's beautiful."

Sasha purred even louder.

"And please, call me Jessica. Mrs. Kendred is what people who don't know me call me, and I think you know me some now."

"That's fine," Emma said. "Mariah, take Bella and Sasha downstairs while I talk with Mrs. . . . Jessica. We will be down to join you after we have had a chance to get to know each other more and I answer her questions."

Mariah did as she was told, leaving the two alone.

Emma's interview went well, and she answered all of Jessica's questions. After a significant amount of time discussing the baker's life, living situation, and financials, Jessica stood up and smiled.

"I think that about does it," she said. "It is plain to me that this arrangement you have made for Mariah is a good one, a safe one, and a nurturing one. My recommendation is that she be allowed to be placed in your care temporarily until all conditions of foster care are met. You mentioned you would be willing to foster Mariah in hopes of adopting her at some point." She paused and looked directly into Emma's eyes. "Is that correct?"

"Yes. Yes, of course," Emma replied.

"Good. Well, let me explain further. It's a long process, with a series of requirements and conditions that must be met. From what I have learned about you in my time here and from interviews with people in this community, you are known for helping others. There will be background checks, classes, forms, and a number of other steps that must be completed. But I'm confident you'll get there, and my recommendation that Mariah be allowed to stay, conditional on meeting all the requirements, will help you get started."

Emma smiled through the tears welling in her eyes. "May I hug you?" she asked Jessica.

"Of course, but only if you'll allow me to hug you back. Now, let's go share the news with Mariah."

"Yes. Yes," Emma said. "Knowing her, she's on pins and needles, impatient and worrying."

"Well, I think most of her worries are taken care of," Jessica said. "Next will be enrolling her in school as soon as possible. I will, of course, assist you with this and the other steps."

It was midafternoon when the caseworker left the two. Seconds after the goodbyes had been spoken, Mariah ran over and hugged Emma so tightly she lost her breath.

"Well now!" Emma said. "I think we have cause for celebration. Put your jacket on. We're going shopping. Shopping for new clothes, school clothes, fun clothes, and the like."

And celebrate they did, with a whirlwind shopping spree where Mariah and Emma chose all manner of clothes and accessories, including a perfect, red French beret. Modeling it in the mirror, Mariah clapped her hands in approval. "Oh, it's just like that raspberry beret that the singer Prince sang about," she told Emma.

They laughed and smiled widely so much during the outing that their faces hurt. The shopping was followed by pizza and ice cream before they returned to the house.

They spread the new clothes all over the tables and floors in Emma's bedroom, admiring their finds. Emma collapsed into a wingback easy chair with Sasha at her feet, and Mariah curled up on one of the couches with Bella tucked in her arms.

The four fell fast asleep, dreaming of what the future held for them.

4

With a yawn and a stretch, Emma was the first to wake as sunlight beamed into her bedroom. She gently shook Mariah on the sofa.

"Good morning, Miss Sleepy," she said softly. "Time for you to go downstairs and get cleaned up while I do the same. I'll come down and make us breakfast and some goodies in the bakery. We can eat there. See you in a bit."

Once she made her way to the bakery, Mariah breathed in the warm, rich smells of cinnamon rolls, eggs, and bacon. The morning sun was warm as it filtered through the tall, curtained windows. Sasha rested beside her saucer of milk, and Bella rested on her blankets in the corner, obviously full from her morning meal.

"Well, Mariah, it's certainly been a wild week," Emma started when the both were seated at the small table. "It's the beginning of a new life for us both, and it's time we give thanks."

Mariah had prayed before, lots of times. They bowed heads with every meal, before bed, and at the beginning of family meetings at the Campbell home. But those prayers were a ritual, a habit, a mandatory reciting of words, a have to, not a want to. So far in her life, religion had been an expected custom and little else. Oh, there was lots of preaching and singing, but it didn't really mean anything to Mariah. Watching Emma put her hands together and lean on her elbows on the table with her eyes closed was entirely different.

"Thank you, Lord of Lords, God of hosts, Creator of all. Thank you for bringing Mariah and me together. Thank you for making it happen that she can stay. Thank you for Bella and Sasha and our friends. Please continue to bless us. Amen."

"Amen," Mariah replied, then paused before continuing. "I didn't know you were religious, Emma."

"Oh, I'm not religious, dear. I leave that for the pastors and preachers and priests and all those that need those things. I am just, as Mr. McCurdy would call himself, a grateful servant of the Most High who recognizes and knows that the universe was created with cause. A grateful servant who knows giving thanks for the blessings and goodness that come from on high is the right thing to do."

"Are you a Christian?" Mariah asked meekly.

"Yes, I guess you could term me so. Mr. McCurdy was raised Catholic, and that seemed to work for him. I was raised Baptist, then changed to Methodist, and later to no specific denomination. Michael and I came to know that God is everywhere and involved in everything. His hands hold all, and love above all things is what is expected of us in return. So, Mariah, how you relate to God or choose to worship him will be your choice to make. Just know one of our obligations in life is to help others, to honor all life forms, and to make better where and when we can. That's the whole point of all my businesses, my work, my life. Now, little one, help with the dishes. After we clean things up, there is someone else important you have yet to meet."

Puzzled, Mariah just smiled and jumped to her feet to start cleaning.

They worked together effortlessly. When they

finished drying the last dish, Emma shooed her out. "Go get dressed, and I'll meet you at the bottom of the stairs. And wear your beret with the new jeans and yellow blouse. Color is one of the things he likes."

"He?" Mariah asked. "Who's he?"

"Oh, you'll see." Emma flashed a curious smile. "Make it quick. The shop opens at ten on Sundays."

"Shop? What shop, Emma?"

"Go on. Enough questions. See you in a bit."

Emma and Mariah left the building through the back entrance and then walked around the side to find a storefront with a multicolored sign. Its paisley scripted letters spelled out *EMMA'S ODDITY EMPORIUM—BOOKS, COLLECTIBLES, AND CURIOSITIES*.

Upon entering through the heavy, ancient-looking wooden and brass door, Emma was immediately welcomed by a high-pitched sing-song voice. "Ah, come in! Come in, Memsahib, mistress of learning and gracious giving. And who, Memsahib, is this little miss beside you?"

Emma smiled as she reached down to hug a

stick-thin, elderly man wearing a threadbare Edwardian suitcoat and pinstriped trousers that looked as old as he was. The attire hung over his wrinkled bronze skin like laundry on a drying rack. He smiled up at Emma.

"She is our family's newest addition," Emma proclaimed joyfully. "Her name is Mariah. She has recently come to live with me. Mariah, this is Vihaan, this shop's manager and another dear friend."

"Welcome. Welcome, little miss," Vihaan said with a low, courteous bow. "So, you, I assume, have come like iron drawn to the magnet of goodness and mercy that is Memsahib Emma. I, too, am a lucky one, having been saved, restored, and given an esteemed place here. Come and sit here, and I will quickly tell you of the event."

He offered Mariah a high-backed cane stool that sat beside the sales counter. For Emma, he pulled out a sturdy chair beside a small table. Then, like a flash, he produced a tray of tea cups and a teapot. He poured a drink for each them that smelled exotic and delicious.

"It's jasmine tea," he said proudly. "Now to the story, Miss, uhh . . ."

"Mariah," Emma replied.

"Ah yes, Miss Mariah. Well, you see, I had been tossed about in the churning sea of circumstance, for a time, when I sought refuge under the portico of this store one rainy night. Curling up like a cat, I covered myself as best I could with my clothes and cardboard before falling asleep. Sahib McCurdy found me the next morning. He brought me inside, gave me work, and offered this splendid suit that had been his years before. And here I am and have been ever since. I manage and care for this magical place full of treasures and delights. And yes"—Vihaan leaned in close to Mariah and whispered in her ear—"it is indeed magical, miss. You will see. You will see."

He smiled with obvious delight. "And Memsahib, where is my Sasha, the sacred all-knowing cat?"

"She is upstairs with another new family member, Mariah's small dog, Bella, whom you will like as much as Sasha."

"It is well. It is well, More-eye-ahh." He rolled the name around in his mouth like a piece of Christmas candy. "More-eye-ahh. It is a good name. It means chosen of God. All names have power, little one, just as all things have life. My old name . . . I have forgotten many years ago and left it behind with my old life. My name now, as you have heard, is Vihaan. It means new beginnings, which coming here and joining the Sahib and Memsahib indeed was.

"Now look around, look around," he urged. "Do not be afraid. Be curious, peer, peek, touch, hold, smell, and explore this marvelous shop of wonders. Go on, go on."

Mariah looked to Emma for permission. She nodded. "Yes, Mariah, go ahead and find yourself a treasure here as gift from Vihaan and me. Find something that catches your eye, but more importantly, something that calls out to you."

"Agreed," Vihaan said solemnly. "Wise words. Here, we have everything from all corners of the world: books, new and ancient; glass suncatchers and bottles; animal skeletons; incense and fragrances from afar; cinnabar; frankincense; antiques of all types; parasols; paintings; tools and musical instruments; even a stuffed monkey's paw, like in the storybook. Magic items of all sizes and types, mirrors, and much more. Explore while Memsahib and I catch up on last week's visitors and business. It has been busy, to that I can attest."

He gave a toothy grin. After smiling back sweetly at Vihaan and Emma, Mariah took a deep breath and wandered about the shop, up one aisle and down another, pausing here and there to pick up an object or trinket. She'd hold the item, then put it back down when there was no spark. Mariah marveled at the treasures from all different parts of the world. In every nook and cranny, there were treats for the eyes and the soul.

Colorful scarves, unique perfumes, books on many subjects, globes made of alabaster, small statues, beads, baubles, drawings, and paintings framed and unframed. Every shelf held a different assortment.

Mariah explored peacefully until she suddenly stopped, as if instructed by some unseen hand. Directly in front of her, sitting on a shelf surrounded by geodes and minerals, she spied a small, round pendant hung from a red cord. Mariah leaned in to examine it. It seemed to be metal with inscriptions and images carved around its edges in some unknown language.

In the very center was a beautiful, multicolored orgonite crystal that looked like a miniature crystal ball. As if called to do so, Mariah picked it up. It began to feel warm, then warmer, and even seemed to glow. When she brought the stone closer to her eyes, it transformed into an image.

It was the image of Vihaan and Emma seated at a small table, talking and laughing. They both seemed to turn to face her and smile knowingly. It was like watching television or looking at a video reel on a cellphone. Mariah was stunned, but not frightened. Then, as quickly as the image appeared, the crystal returned to its original state.

Mariah stood there for the longest time, holding the pendant in her hands until she felt a presence. She turned to see the toothy smile of Vihaan.

"Ah, I see you have chosen the Amulet of Seeing, as it sometimes called. That amulet with the orgonite . . . some say it can see as an eye can see," he explained. "Well, it is yours and yours to use carefully. It is said the Amulet of Seeing only shows its powers to those fortunate few that are truly pure of heart. To all others, it is nothing more than an attractive pendant. Keep it and use it powers wisely."

Mariah struggled to find her words. "Thank you. It is like nothing I have ever seen before."

Vihaan's smile returned. "It is good that it lets you see its power. For most people, it is not so."

As Emma and Mariah said goodbye, Vihaan bowed to them. "Come again, young miss. Do not be a stranger to this humble shop. Memsahib has told me you are now part of the family. And as family, you and I are now a newly connected piece of the universe."

Back out in the fresh air, Emma decided it was a good day to visit the park. After retrieving Bella and a leash, the ladies headed out.

Bella loved seeing other people and other dogs. She told Mariah this new life was the best life. Mariah leaned down from the bench where she sat with Emma to stroke Bella's fur in agreement.

For the rest of the afternoon after their excursion, Emma napped. Mariah explored the library and music room, where she read and eventually feel asleep listening to Rimsky-Korsakov's beautiful *Scheherazade*. She dreamt she was a princess, captivating the hearts and minds of her people.

5

L ife was good. Mariah enjoyed her new school and the friends she made there. She also liked the teachers who didn't pry or ask too many questions about her background or family. Most, if not all, of her new teachers seemed to admire Mariah's independent spirit, curiosity, and intelligence.

There was one teacher—Ms. Bennington— that Mariah liked and admired most. The English teacher always smiled. She greeted each student by name warmly every day as they entered her classroom, and she seemed especially fond of saying Mariah's name. She stretched out its syllables in a musical sort of way. Ms. Bennington also bragged on Mariah's reading abilities and her natural skill for writing poetry and short stories. She was Mariah's favorite teacher, and her English class was Mariah's favorite class.

Ms. Bennington was known for bringing out the best in her students. One day, when another new student came to class, Ms. Bennington asked Mariah to help her with the class routines and procedures. The two girls became fast friends.

Madison had bright red hair and flashing green eyes, and though she was not knockout pretty, the girl was friendly and down to Earth. She and her divorced mother had recently moved to town. Mariah soon discovered they had many favorites in common, such as Dr Pepper, ravioli, the colors pink and soft blue, reading, and, most of all, music.

Both girls decided to join the school orchestra and take up the violin. They practiced together, studied together, and confided their opinions about life, other students, and boys with each other. Mariah soon introduced Madison to Emma. Sometimes when Madison visited, she helped Mariah with her chores.

Every day, Mariah helped prepare the bakery before Emma drove her to school. Mariah came straight home most days; she liked school and friends her age, but more than anything, she enjoyed Emma's world and her place in it.

She was happy, really happy, for the first time

in her life.

Bella told Mariah that she was happy, too, through the special bond they enjoyed from the beginning. Bella said she liked Sasha and that they spent the day playing, napping, or guarding the home by peering out the windows for would-be dangers.

Winter turned to spring, and Mariah embraced the change by becoming more and more instrumental in Emma's life. The two often ate meals on the weekends at the Café of Hope, Café Esperanza, and from time to time visited Vihaan in the curiosity shop.

Mariah alternated working in those places, sometimes acting as a server or bus girl at the café and other times keeping Vihaan company while dusting the counters, nooks, and crannies of the displays.

"Are you happy here?" Emma asked Mariah one day, her eyes hopeful.

Mariah sat perched high on Emma's stool in the bakery. "Oh, yes! I'm happier than I have ever been in my life. In fact, Emma, I never knew or thought a person could be this happy. It's hard to explain."

"I understand, dear. That was exactly the way I felt every day with my Michael. I'm still happy now, but in a different way. And you have helped reignite that happiness and excitement in my life."

Mariah smiled shyly, then burst out with, "Bella loves it here, too."

"Does she now?" Emma asked with a short laugh.

"Yes, she told me so. And she likes being friends with Sasha."

"Well, truth be known, Sasha says the same of her," Emma said. "Now, let me ask you a question: What do you think you have learned working here in the bakery? Or by being a waitress and helping in the kitchen at the café? Or what have you observed or learned from helping Vihaan?"

"Wow," Mariah pondered. "That's a tough question. I mean, I've learned recipes and such in the bakery, and I've learned how busy a café can be and all the things that have to be done. And with Vihaan, I learned that he cares about his work and likes his job. I love learning more of the mysteries of his Hindu people and the other cultures that he seems to know so much about."

"Yes, yes, that's all true," Emma said. "But let me ask you this another way. Aside from the necessary routines for each, what else have you learned?"

"I don't understand." Mariah felt somewhat ashamed that she hadn't given the answer Emma was hoping for.

"It's tough, Mariah, but let's think. What do all three have in common? I mean, besides the jobs themselves. Whom do the businesses serve?"

"Customers?" Mariah asked meekly.

"Well, yes, customers. But Mariah, who are the customers?"

"Well, people. Just people, I mean."

Emma pulled up a chair and sat next to Mariah. "It's a tough question I have posed for you, I know. And yes, the customers are people. But here's the thing, here's the pearl. They are not 'just people.' Everyone is different, just like you and I are different. Every customer is more than a customer. They are people who have their own lives and dreams, needs and wants, and, in many cases, problems and questions. I'll let you in on a little secret now. Money is important, since it takes money to keep things afloat. My purpose, however, is to be a secret agent."

"A secret agent?" Mariah blurted out, both intrigued and scared by those words.

"Oh, not like James Bond or some spy," Emma laughed. "Maybe those are the wrong words. What I mean is that, from time to time, I observe people who come into the bakery, the café, or the curiosity shop. I watch and learn. I see people in a hurry all the time, obsessed with getting from one place to another. I see men and women, young and old, who don't seem to have any purpose other than getting from Point A to Point B. I see people of all backgrounds who don't seem to be living life as much as they are just existing. They remain in their place of doing this or that, getting this or that, and moving on in a steady stream of sameness."

Mariah watched Emma's expression as she spoke these strange combinations of words. "I don't understand. How does that fit in in with being a secret agent?"

Emma laughed heartily. "Let me slow down and explain better. What I'm trying to get at, what I'm trying to say in my tangled web of words, is this: I want to help those who need it. Every so often, I see a person in a state of worry, or panic, or depression. I seek to be like an angel and guide them."

"But how, Emma? How can you know what they're feeling and how can you help them? I'm sorry, but I still don't understand."

Emma clapped her hands in delight and smiled big at Mariah. "Oh, but you actually do understand! You just explained the two keys. First, how can I know what they're feeling or thinking? Second, how can I help them? Well, here it is. You know how you and Bella communicate through your thoughts, as Sasha does with me? I have learned over the years and honed the ability—limited as it is—to hear, see, and sometimes feel what another person is going through. Scientists call it empathy or telepathy. My dear Michael was incredibly intuitive. He could sense things about people and situations, spot on. He called it listening to his little voices, and he was seldom wrong."

"So being this agent of good," Emma continued, "I use that power of understanding. Actually, one of the reasons I invited you and Bella into my home and into my heart was a result of that very thing. When you first appeared in the alley behind the bakery, I sensed you coming.

It took no special talent to see you were cold, hungry, and obviously on your own. But then, what I heard in your mind was the need for help and the hope that I might be that help. I heard your struggle and, most of all, your fear of what might happen to you. I also understood from your thoughts that you were a good person, yet all alone. That's when I knew I could be that agent of help—secretly, of course. But just as the name of the bakery says, kindness is my goal.

"And every so often, when I see a customer whose soul reaches out, I try to find a way to help. Sometimes, it is to offer them coffee and a listening ear. Sometimes, it is a small gift of money. Other times, I can help by connecting others in the community with that person in need of aid. There are many ways to help someone, but first a helper must determine the need and how to help. And the helper must be sincere; otherwise, the gift of reading someone's mind could be used for evil, selfishness, or deceit. The ability to read minds is a gift, but a gift that is meant to be used for kindness. I think that perhaps you might have some of the same gifts."

"Me? No. I mean, yes," Mariah said. "I can communicate with Bella, but I don't think I have any other ability."

"I think you do," Emma said.

"Vihaan told me about your first encounter with the Amulet of Seeing. He told me you saw he and I seated at the table, smiling back at you."

"But how could he know?" Mariah burst out. "I was seeing you two. I did see you two, but how?"

"Vihaan also has the abilities we spoke of. He can see, just as I can. And now, with the help of the amulet, you can as well. I think the time may come that one day you will have the ability to see without the aid of the amulet, with empathy and telepathy, just as we do. In fact, Mariah, there are ways to practice telepathy, seeing into other's hearts just like you practice with your violin. The more you practice, the better you get. The ability to see into other's desires, fears, and needs is just one more way to be kind, if you use those skills in the right way."

"I'll be happy to teach you and guide you as you learn, if that is what you wish," Emma offered. "Being able to help others by seeing into their thoughts is a special gift and talent, one that requires great care. Mariah, you have that gift. That is another reason you are so special. It is your gift, if you claim it."

Mariah was stunned, too stunned to answer. In the meantime, Emma listened to her mind and her heart.

"Oh, dear one, do not be afraid. It is a gift from God, and as the late Mr. McCurdy often would say, what talents we have are God's gifts to us, and what we do with those talents is our gift back to God. Use your gifts wisely and, above all, use your gifts for good. Promise me that, Mariah."

Mariah took hold of Emma's hand and looked deep into her eyes. "I understand, and I will. I will," Mariah said as if it was a promise, which indeed it was.

6

Mariah couldn't, wouldn't, tell anyone about her gift, including Madison. Still, she was determined to practice and learn the methods that Emma laid out, including meditation, focusing deeply on objects, being quiet to shut out distractions, and listening while seeing. That last skill was the hardest, tuning into another person's thoughts or emotions with eyes and ears. But it worked.

One day, while all the students were reading silently in Ms. Bennington's English class, Mariah decided to practice. She slowed her breathing, squinted her eyes, and opened her mind like a radar beam that pulled her focus to Madison. Without a word, Madison's thoughts and intense sorrow enveloped her. Mariah didn't know what to do, so she just kept breathing slowly in and out. She shut her eyes momentarily, and an image appeared like a phone screen tapped on.

The blurry images slowly came into focus.

"Of course I love you, Madison, but your mom and I no longer love each other like we did in the past. It's not working."

"Daddy, don't say that. Mom still loves you. I still love you. Please, please, please don't go. Don't get divorced."

"Madison, listen to me." The man's voice grew stronger and somewhat impatient. *"I'm doing what's best for you, for Margaret, and for me, too. One day, you'll understand. But for now, I've got to go and that's it. I'll still make time to see you, but I can't stay here any longer. And that's final."*

Mariah watched as the images blurred again. A whirring noise, like the buzz of a mosquito or a rush of wind, caught her off-guard.

"Mariah, close your book. . . . Mariah!" Ms. Bennington's voice grew stronger and somewhat insistent. "I can't believe you, of all people, were daydreaming in my class. I hope you are finished because it's time to review for the exam on Wednesday."

Suddenly becoming aware, Mariah's breaths came quickly. Her pulse quickened, her focus widened like the eye of a camera, and she was back in the present. "I'm sorry, Ms. Bennington. I guess I'm just tired."

"Well, that's okay, but you kind of worried me. Like, you were in a trance or something. It's not like you to zone out."

"No, ma'am," Mariah answered apologetically. "I'm sorry."

"I'm just glad you're okay, but now we need to move on." Ms. Bennington moved from row to row, handing out the study guides.

As Mariah looked up to take her copy, she spotted an almost-undetectable tear in Madison's eyes. Her friend quickly wiped it away, then put the study guide up close to her face to hide any emotion she might betray. It was then that Mariah knew she had *seen*. Mariah knew she could see, and if this gift was hers, she must be very careful with how and when she used it. Most of all, Mariah knew that if she did use it, she must use the gift in the right way, as Emma had instructed her. Seeing was a way to help others, after all.

That night, Mariah told Emma what happened at school—the sights, feelings, and all that she experienced. Emma, seated next to her, took

Mariah's hand gently and looked into her eyes.

"Yes, wonderful!" Emma said. "I knew you were special and that you held special gifts, with the potential for even more. But, most of all, I knew you had a good heart and good intentions toward all of God's creatures. Mariah, that is the most important lesson: To not only feel for others, but, if possible, to find a way to reach out or to make the world a better place."

Mariah grinned back at her. "Emma, I have so much to learn and so much I want to learn."

"And you will dear," Emma said. "But in the meantime, let's show extra kindness and warmth to Madison."

That night, Mariah dreamed about her old life and the do-gooders with their rigid rules. That good, that impact, was limited. With Emma, there was no limit to doing good, authentic good. Mariah believed there was no challenge too big or small for Emma's love and good intentions. The next morning would prove otherwise, though.

The sun wasn't quite up, but Mariah was. As usual on weekdays, she helped Emma and a volunteer remove freshly baked goods from the ovens and prepare them for the glass display cases. It was Monday morning, and like most Monday mornings, Emma had errands to run. There was the usual bank visit, a quick drop-in to the neighborhood pharmacy for medication refills and other items, and other tasks that varied by the week. On this particular Monday, Emma had scheduled a checkup for Sasha with his veterinarian.

"I should be back shortly before noon, Helen," Emma told her friend and longtime bakery helper. "Mariah will help you until seven-thirty when she catches the bus to school."

She gave Mariah a quick kiss on her cheek. "Take care of things and help Helen. Have a great day, and learn as much as you can. But mainly"—Emma paused and leaned down to whisper into Mariah's ear—"have some fun, hon. It's one of life's rewards."

Emma grabbed her purse and rushed toward the hallway, but turned back for just a moment. "And be kind, both of you. This is a kind house bakery, right?"

"Right," Helen and Mariah cheerfully replied.

Emma hadn't been gone for more than a few

minutes when Mariah heard banging on the front door.

"Let me in! Let me in this instant!" An angry woman's high-pitched voice echoed against the glass of the storefront. The tall, agitated visitor appeared to be in her sixties or early seventies, sporting bright red hair, a dull black dress, and a black coat draped over one arm. What appeared to be a small notebook was clutched tightly in her hand.

After easing the front door open a crack, the frightened Mariah managed a meager smile. "Sorry, ma'am. We're not quite ready yet. We open at seven, and it's just now six-thirty. We have lots to do before we open to the public."

The imposing woman pushed against the door with all her might and barged right in. "Well, I'm not the public, and it's a disgrace that a bakery can't be ready to open for its customers at peak morning time."

Taking out her notebook, the woman scribbled down complaints. "And another thing: The sidewalk out front needs to be swept. And the outside lights should be on."

Helen rushed over from behind the counter,

standing protectively in front of Mariah. "Madam, we will be happy to serve you, though we're not quite officially open," she said calmly. "How can we help you?"

The woman's voice was loud and dismissive. "You can help me by bringing me some tea or coffee, assuming you have the brains to do so." Her face contorted into a scowl as she flopped down in the small chair at a table near the door.

"Where's Emma?" she demanded as she opened her notebook in front of her. "Surely, she's here."

Mariah quickly brought the woman a cup of coffee and offered sugar and cream. The woman sniffed the cream, took two heaping spoons of sugar, then stirred her cup furiously.

"What a waste, serving sugar in a bowl. How wasteful. You should use sugar packets like everybody else. Wasteful, no sugar packets," she said as she wrote it down. "Where's Emma?"

"She's not here," Mariah said. "She will be back later today. Can I be of help?"

"I doubt it. I doubt you or this woman can be any kind of help. When will Emma be back *exactly*? Don't hem and haw or beat around the bush."

Mariah's eyes narrowed, and she spoke without thinking. "Excuse me, but who are you and what business do you have with Emma?"

"I am Judith McCurdy Bleary. That's who. And this business is my business, and none of your business. Let me make this clear at the outset: I am part-owner of this and the other McCurdy businesses, and I'm here to make my assessment and protect my interests in these operations. And you, young lady, and your coworker would be wise to learn that at the get-go. Now, go and get this bakery ready for customers." She looked at her watch. "According to your operating hours, you have exactly eight minutes to get things right before you open the doors. I will take my coffee here and watch as the customers arrive. Bear in mind, I will be watching you and taking notes."

Helen straightened her apron. After unsuccessfully attempting to shake the woman's hand, she managed a smile. "Well, it's nice to meet you. I am Helen Carter, and this is Mariah McCurdy."

Judith took her glasses from her purse and placed them on the bridge of her nose. She squinted at Mariah, her eyes cold and hard.

"Mariah McCurdy? I don't know you, and Emma has no children. Of that, I am certain. Who are you, young lady, and why are you using the McCurdy name? Answer me immediately," she demanded.

"Emma took me in and adopted me. She gave me her last name," Mariah said.

"Oh, she did, did she? Well, this is the first I've heard of this nonsense. And just what do you do here?"

Mariah was both hurt and angry. "I live here. I work here. Emma's my . . ."

But before she could go on, Helen gently redirected her. "Mariah, go on and get ready for school. I'll handle things here until Emma gets back. Don't worry about us."

Helen had barely gotten those words out when customers started streaming through the doors. Mariah looked at the customers and then back at Helen, but did as she was told. "I'll be back just as soon as school is out. I'll be back."

Helen regained her composure and attempted smiles as customers filed in, sometimes one at a time and other times six or seven at once.

Helen warmly greeted each one, sometimes calling regular customers by their names. All the while, Judith the intruder glared from her seat and furiously scribbled notes.

After about an hour, when the morning rush momentarily subsided, Helen retreated to the kitchen to call Emma on her cellphone.

Emma was leaving the bank when she saw the bakery number on her Caller ID. Concerned, she immediately answered. "Helen, what's wrong? Is there a fire or something? Why are you calling?"

Helen broke in. "Emma, come home now. There's a woman here claiming she is a McCurdy and owns part of the bakery. She has parked herself at a table and seems to be evaluating me, and . . . oh, Emma."

"Calm down, Helen. I'll head there immediately. Just go about your work, and I'll deal with this. Thank you for calling me. Stay calm. Everything will be all right."

"But do you know who this is, Emma?"

"I'm sure it's Michael's sister," she replied calmly. "I'll explain more when we get a chance to talk. For now, just smile and try to ignore her until I get there."

"Okay, Emma, but hurry. Please, hurry."

A few minutes later, Emma had returned. She quickly took Sasha upstairs before greeting the persnickety woman. "Well, Judith, this is a surprise. What brings you here from Pennsylvania?"

"My inheritance, that's what. Or what's left of it," her sister-in-law replied. "From what I've seen, you run a loose ship, Emma. You always were soft-hearted, if not soft-headed."

Emma held up her hand like a traffic cop stopping an oncoming car, or a teacher stopping an out-of-control third-grader. "Enough, Judith. Let's go upstairs and talk. Not here, in front of customers and such. Come on upstairs with me."

"Now see here, Emma! You have no right to boss me around—"

Emma cut her off. "I have every right to ask you to calm down and sit down with me privately where we can catch up and address your concerns."

"Concerns are right. If my ten percent of the business is being run into the ground, then I have every right to try to correct it."

"Upstairs, Judith. Now," Emma commanded with a stern tone Helen hadn't heard before.

What followed over coffee and the next half-hour was a long stream of disjointed tidbits from Judith's recent struggles. Her husband of forty years died suddenly of a heart attack last month, leaving Judith with little. When all was said and done, his estate only included their old house in disrepair (now sold), two older-model cars (one sold), and a modest bank account. There was no life insurance and no children or other heirs. It was just Judith and her two cats, which she promptly surrendered to the local animal shelter. She was alone and had enough funds from her retirement with Sandy Oaks Savings and Loan to live modestly, if not frugally.

"So, in short, I moved here. I have rented a small apartment on Twenty-seventh Street, not far from here, in the Fleetwood area."

Emma spoke for the first time since they arrived upstairs. "I know that area."

"Well, since I have no full-time job, nor do I want one, I have made a decision to spend my time monitoring and guiding Emerald Enterprises, of which, I remind you, Michael left me ten percent."

"You don't need to remind me of that," Emma replied. "It was something Michael and I both agreed to. Though he and you were never really close, he still couldn't fathom not giving you something, since you were his sister. Now, I am prepared to pay you off in one lump sum. Ten percent of roughly six hundred thousand is sixty thousand."

"You'll do no such thing!" Judith exclaimed. "I'll not be bought off that easily. No sirree, Bob. I may be older than you, but I'm not fool. No, I'll retain my ten percent and, with my help, make it grow."

"Let me be blunt," Emma said. "I don't want you interfering in the businesses, my businesses, and my life. I don't want you snooping around, day in and day out, and I don't want your advice. Have I made myself clear?"

"Words, words, dear Emma, but your words can't stop me from what is mine. Now, if you'll excuse me, I have an appointment with a lawyer. I have written down my phone number, address, and such for you downstairs."

Judith practically scurried to the door. Emma stood alone in her apartment, too stunned to react.

7

J udith popped in and out of the bakery on different days and times as she pleased and even demanded Helen show her the kitchen, ovens, and procedures. Emma would call Judith once she found out about each visit, and the two would argue to no end.

Judith was rude, crude, cruel, and offensive to everyone, not just the employees. She caused a scene when she slipped into Café Esperanza, posing as a regular customer. After scrutinizing the menu for the longest time, she scoffed at Veronica. "Do you serve anything other than this warmed-over Mexican trash?"

Veronica didn't know what to say. She stood there frozen until Mateo came to the table and politely asked if he could help.

"I repeat, do you serve anything other than this garbage mish-mash you call Mexican food?"

Judith eyed Mateo with undisguised scorn. "It's bad enough that we allow you immigrants into our country, but then to have to pay for this poor excuse for food is ridiculous."

Veronica's eyes filled with tears at the insults. Mateo gently hugged her waist and sent her back to the kitchen. "I'm sorry, Señora, if you don't like our offerings. I guarantee you all items are authentic and prepared with care and from age-old family recipes."

"Well," Judith huffed, "if you're going to make a profit, you'll have to do better than this. I suggest you learn to cook and offer real American food here as well, such as burgers, steaks, spaghetti, seafood, and the rest. How can you call yourself a restaurant if this is what you call food?" she asked as she pointed to a plate of enchiladas at the table next to hers. "Besides, it is obviously way too spicy. A person can't eat more than one meal of this a month, and that isn't enough to support a business or grow one."

Mateo took a deep breath. "Señora, I will happily bring you a sample on the house before you order, or you are welcome to go elsewhere."

"Free food? No, you fool! Now you're just throwing away money, and as a part-owner, I'll not have it."

"Part . . . owner?" Mateo asked, struggling with the words. "But this restaurant is owned by Miss Emma."

"Mrs. Emma McCurdy," Judith broke in, "and I am Judith McCurdy Bleary, her sister-in-law. My late brother left me a portion of Emerald Enterprises, of which this . . . *restaurant* is but one part. I intend to see my investment is handled wisely. A business is not a charity, and helping immigrants is not part of a good business model. And that young woman, my waitress, even has an accent like you. Really? Perhaps she doesn't understand American customers well."

"That young woman is my daughter," Mateo said, his voice rising. "And my daughter, Veronica, is about to be a college graduate and will be entering the medical field next year. Her accent is part of her culture, of which she and I are very proud."

"Well, your culture doesn't mean much to me if your menu is limited and the food is average at best," Judith shot back.

"Señora, part-owner or not, I must ask you to not insult us. I will discuss the visit with Miss

Emma. Now, please leave."

Judith was the one left stunned for once. She slammed down her napkin, picked up her purse, and stormed out the door. "You haven't heard the last from me!" she shouted.

"Madre de Dios, protect us from such a Diabla," Mateo whispered under his breath.

Things went no better when Judith marched into Emma's Oddity Emporium. Vihaan sat quietly on his stool, stroking Sasha's fur. The cat often visited to sleep in a miniature Egyptian throne, basking in the warmth of the sunlight coming through the window.

The part-owner shoved the door open forcefully, almost knocking off the attached bell. Before Vihaan could welcome her, Judith began jotting notes in her little book. "Dust, dust everywhere. Low lighting. Customers can't see well," she muttered as she walked up and down aisles, picking up and setting down item after item.

Vihaan, almost running, finally caught up with her. "Good day, madam, and welcome. Can I be of some assistance?"

"Assistance? I think not. You are obviously the

one needing assistance. And who might you be?"

Bowing slowly, Vihaan smiled at her. "I am Vihaan, keeper of the treasures here at Emma's Oddity Emporium."

"Keeper of the treasures?" Judith asked. "I see no treasures here, only recycled junk and crap from garage sales or secondhand stores."

"Oh no, madam, treasures there are. Many old and specialty items. Allow me to show—"

"I have no need for you to show me anything," Judith snapped. "I'll have you know, Vincent or whatever your name is, that I am Judith McCurdy Bleary, and my late brother Michael McCurdy left me part-ownership of this junk store, along with other properties and investments."

"Oh, I see," Vihaan's wheels spun as he assessed the situation. One of his many talents was pulling pieces together and solving things quickly. "Well then, welcome, Memsahib Judith. I am at your service. You are then sister-in-law to Miss Emma, yes?"

"That's right, technically," Judith said. "But enough of explanations. It is what they say it is, and I am who I am. Now Vincent, let's talk turkey."

"Turkey, Memsahib? I don't understand."

"Don't be cagey with me, you little Hindu or whatever you are. I want to know how much inventory is kept versus how much weekly or monthly sales are. Do I make myself clear?"

"You do, indeed. But those are questions for Emma, Mrs. McCurdy, not a backwards humble servant as myself. If you'll excuse me, I'll go back to my duties."

"Do that," Judith replied harshly. "Oh, and get that cat out of this store immediately. A pet has no place in a business."

"But Memsahib, that cat is Mrs. McCurdy's and often visits with her permission."

"Really? Well, all that will change soon enough. And one more thing: Don't call me memsahib or whatever. You'll henceforth address me as Mrs. Bleary, understood?"

Vihaan stood silent, taken aback at her tone.

"Are you hard of hearing as well as stupid? It's Mrs. Bleary, understood?"

"Understood," Vihaan said as he bowed and walked backward toward the counter.

He sat glued to his stool for the remainder of her thirty-minute visit, saying nothing as Judith prowled around giving notes and angry comments. Sometimes, Judith just smacked her gums, making a squeaking noise like a mouse. Other times, she seemed to snort or snicker like a horse. She finally left, slamming the door behind her.

That night, a council of sorts convened in Emma's apartment. Emma's family—Helen, Mariah, Mateo, Veronica, Delores, and Vihaan—gathered around a large, round table. At their feet were the curled figures of Sasha and Bella, who were just as much a part of the family as the others. Bella and Sasha looked at each other and spoke their silent language until their human counterparts did with words.

The people all sat there, glancing nervously at the others and waiting for someone to be the first to speak. Each anxiously looked across the table at one another. Mariah wanted to talk, to say what was on her mind, but she hesitated with respect for the grownups. Vihaan breathed in and out loudly, trying to calm himself. Mateo closed his eyes, as if in prayer, saying nothing. Veronica and Delores sat silent. Helen fidgeted, constantly folding and then unfolding her hands.

Finally, it was Emma who broke the silence. "We have a problem. Well, *problems*, actually, but the problems all originate with my sister-in-law, Judith."

"Oh yes, Memsahib," Vihaan broke in. "She is badness, that one. I see and feel it. I look into her heart, which is dark as night. She comes into the shop only to complain about this and that and always about how bad I am as a salesman. As you know, Memsahib, I am not a salesman. I am a curator, a historian, and yes, a purveyor of collectibles and such, but much more. The shop makes money, yes, but it is not a grocery store or a used car lot where I try to be as pushy as Miss Judith wants. It hurts my soul, honestly, I tell you. It hurts my soul to be accused of being lazy or unfaithful to you."

Emma nodded her head and reached across the table to take Vihaan's hands. She gently kissed them. "You have always been a blessing, dear Vihaan, and never a burden or a problem."

Helen spoke up next. "The problem is that woman. I mean no disrespect to your family. As the saying goes, we can choose our friends, but not our family. But Emma, she scares the chickens, constantly complains that the chicken feed we use is too expensive, gripes about our supplies and the price of eggs and other ingredients. She says we shouldn't heat the bakery and just let the heat of the ovens do the work, but the customers get cold in front. That woman insists I and the others call her Mrs. Bleary, like she's the queen of Sheba, which she isn't. Honestly, Emma, I don't know how much longer I and the others can take it. She's mean, harsh, unpleasant, and well, just a witch, if you pardon my language."

Mariah laughed, breaking the sullen mood at the table. "I agree, Helen. I think Miss Judith is a three-way villain: Part Cruella de Vil, part Evil Queen from *Snow White*, and, most of all, the Wicked Witch of the West. I have nightmares of her pointing a finger at me and saying, "I'll get you, my pretty! You and that little dog, too."

Bella yelped loudly from her place under the table. Sasha rubbed up against Emma's leg. Emma reached down to pet Sasha, then looked to Mateo. "Well, dear friend, we haven't heard from your family yet. Share with us what's on your heart and mind. I . . . we all need to know."

Mateo opened his eyes and spoke deliberately and evenly. "All we have heard is true. I will only add . . ."

He paused to look at his daughter and then at his tearful wife. "Yes, all we have heard and experienced these things, it is true. Mrs. Bleary treats all of us as her servants and, even then, not in a kind way. I will not list the problems or happenings, just to say this from my language and my people: El que se enoja piende."

They all stared at Mateo and then at each other, as if expecting someone to know the meaning of the words. Sasha curled up next to Bella, who looked into the cat's eyes for understanding.

Mateo let the words hang in the air momentarily before he translated. "It means, 'The one who gets mad loses.' I think, dear friends and familia, we must not get mad or make decisions based on anger."

Helen spoke up. "Those are kind words, Mateo, but we need action."

The others nodded their heads, except Emma. She reached out and took Mateo's hands into her own.

"No, Mateo is right," Emma said. "I talked to my attorney and others, and I floated the idea of obtaining a restraining order or order of no contact to bar Judith from our premises. They all told me that was not a lasting remedy, and that, even if approved, it would only be temporary at best. She does own one-tenth of each business, after all. Our only recourse is to be patient, show kindness, and hope for a change of heart in Judith. We can pray. We can meditate. We can show compassion. We can hope that the forces of good in the universe will come to our aid."

Emma looked at each person gathered at the table as she finished. They all joined hands and silently agreed.

8

One Sunday afternoon, Emma and Mariah arranged to visit Judith in her small apartment, using the excuse they needed her to sign some papers for the company's insurance policy. The real truth, as Emma confided to Mariah, was to find common ground.

"We need to see if we can become closer to Judith. More importantly, we need to see if we can get Judith to become more of an ally to us than the adversary she is now."

Mariah agreed. "Do you think we can maybe learn something about Judith?"

"What do you mean?" Emma asked curiously.

"Well, you know, maybe we can use our gifts, our telepathy, to find the source of her meanness. Maybe then we could even find a way to help her or change her."

"Maybe. Maybe," Emma repeated hopefully under her breath.

After they knocked at the door, Judith opened it just a smidge. "Oh, it's you," she said. "Well, come in, but let's make this quick. If it's business, fine, but nothing more. No cutesy socializing."

She noticed Mariah standing behind Emma, then let out a scoff. "Why did you bring her along? This is supposed to be a business meeting."

Emma entered the small living room. "Mariah has every reason to be here," she replied curtly. "She is part-owner as well, by virtue of being my adopted daughter and may—no, will—inherit Emerald Enterprises one day."

"We'll see about that," Judith said.

"Indeed, we will." Emma smiled. "Indeed, we will."

Judith's apartment was sparse and utilitarian. It had a simple kitchen with a small table, two chairs, and an open cupboard showing one plate and two bowls. The home also had a couch, two living room recliners, a coffee table, and a dining room table with a well-worn plastic tablecloth and one chair. One end of the living room was dominated by a massive rolltop desk covered in piles of neatly stacked papers, some ink pens, and a mostly empty tin can that held mechanical pencils. There were blinds over the windows, but no curtains. There was no real decor or artwork on the walls, only a few framed photos of Judith and her late husband that Mariah guessed were taken when they were young, and a photo of a weather-beaten wooden house and barn. Even the kitchen refrigerator was stark white and bare of the usual magnets.

"Mrs. Bleary, could I please use the bathroom?" Mariah asked.

Judith grunted and tilted her head toward a short hallway. As Mariah walked to the bathroom, she peeked into Judith's bedroom. She tiptoed in while listening for the back-and-forth voices of Emma and Judith. They discussed the bakery, the restaurant, and, most of all, Vihaan, who from the tone of conversation was Judith's main nemesis.

Mariah looked around quickly. She saw a dressing table with a few beauty items, an open clothes closet, a mirrored chest of drawers, and a twin bed with a threadbare quilt on top. Next to the bed, a nightstand held a single framed photo that drew Mariah in like a magnet.

After scanning the room once more to see if she'd been spotted, Mariah held up the framed image of a small girl, probably about five or six years old, sitting in a rocking chair and fiercely clutching a doll or toy animal.

Mariah felt the powerful energy the photo seemed to contain. In came a flood of emotions—happiness, warmth, sadness, regret, hurt, and loneliness most of all. Before dizziness fully set in, she forced herself to put the photo back on the table and to finally visit the bathroom.

When Mariah returned to the living room, she saw Emma folding the papers she had brought to show Judith. "Well, I am glad you agree with the insurance policy and premiums," Emma said as she stood to leave. "Thank you."

"It is as it has to be, unfortunately," Judith replied. "I don't like it, and, as a rule, I don't believe in insurance at all. But in the case of the buildings, the business, and the way things are today in our society, I just know it's like putting gas in the car or changing the oil. I don't like it, but you have to have it. Now, is there anything else?"

"No, that's it, but why don't you join Mariah and I for dinner one evening? Or, we can dine out, if you would rather."

"I'd rather not do either. I'm fine here, and dining out, as you call it, is simply extravagant. Food is fuel, nothing more and nothing less."

"Oh, come on!" Emma said. "Wouldn't you like to just have a treat now and then? A little indulgence is good for the soul."

"Ridiculous. A treat!" Judith flung the words back. "Indulgence is just that. If it's not a necessity, then it's unnecessary. Now, if you'll excuse me, I'll bid you both goodbye."

Mariah looked at Emma, who bowed her head in defeat as they walked out the door. Driving back home, neither said a word until moments before they arrived.

"Oh Emma, Judith is so sad," Mariah told her. "I wonder if she's been sad all her life. And I wonder what made her sad, and I wonder if there's anything that can make her happy."

Emma looked over and smiled at Mariah. "Who knows? Perhaps. And if there is, I hope more than hope that Judith can find it again."

Nothing changed, though. Everything remained very much the same with Judith. Helen, Mateo, Veronica, Deloris, Vihaan, Emma, and Mariah were still the source of her displeasure.

Over the next few months, Judith made it a point to become more and more involved in the businesses. Judith would march into the bakery at the first sign of light, constantly scribbling notes of every mistake or imagined infraction she saw. She constantly belittled Helen and Emma for donating leftover baked goods to the homeless or local charities. Her favorite words were wasteful, wasteful, and wasteful. "That's money out of our pockets," she'd say on repeat.

And then there were Judith's complaints about the chickens. She insisted over and over and over again that the chickens were being fed too often. "Chickens are like pigs," she'd say during her rants. "They can live on scraps. That feed costs too much. And here's another thing: I insist that the chickens be killed and eaten when they quit producing eggs. This is not a charity house, and God forbid it should ever become one. Kind House Bakery, indeed. Wasting money is not kind; it's just stupid. And being kind never got anyone any money."

It didn't stop there. Judith constantly instructed Veronica to reuse or serve leftover food, or even place it in plastic containers for Judith to take home with her. Judith had her nose in everything, and it bothered Delores to no end that Judith would watch her in the kitchen. She would scold her for not using measuring cups or making customer portions too big. She yelled at Mateo for not pushing customers out the door after a meal and instead allowing them to linger and talk.

And Vihaan, poor Vihaan, was treated the worst. Constantly, Judith would insult or shame him, call him That Hindu, and berate him over his use of old phrases or antiquated images. She would thrust a dust cloth or feather duster into his hands, demanding he be useful. Judith also didn't like many of the items for sale, and she urged Vihaan often to sell more modern items.

"Nobody cares about antiques or garage sale leftovers," she told him.

Vihaan would always bow, nod politely, and stifle the hurt he felt. It was no longer a privilege or joy to do this work; it no longer seemed like his home away from home. It had become a prison of sorts, and the jailer, Mrs. Bleary, was harsh and unrelenting.

On thankfully rare days, Judith, who usually ignored animals, directed her wrath toward Bella and Sasha. When Bella approached her and offered a stuffed toy, Judith kicked it aside. "Stay out from under my feet, you useless mutt," she scolded.

Sasha eyed Judith, but wisely kept her distance. Judith didn't hesitate to make it known she had no use for cats either. "Cats are such useless animals, constantly preening and lazing about. Just another waste of time and money."

It was impossible to escape Judith's scrutiny. She became more cutting and aggressively snide to Mariah over time. "Listen young lady, you should brush your hair more and talk less," she barked. "You should study more and be of more help to our businesses, instead of wasting your time learning and paying good money for violin lessons. Music is a luxury, and wasteful luxuries are not good for business or the pocketbook. And I'll tell you another thing," Judith said pointing her finger in Mariah's face, "I'd advise you when you become of legal age to earn your own way, signing back to Emerald Enterprises all you've been promised as a way of repaying

Emma and the company for all the years you lived on Emma's charity."

Yet, they all endured. Emma, Helen, Mateo, Veronica, Delores, Mariah, and even Vihaan. They remained strong because they loved their work, they loved this family stitched together by Emma, and, most of all, they loved the magic of their lives before Judith had crashed down like a meteor. *No,* Mariah thought, *it was more like a disease that had infected them, but they didn't know the cure.* So, each did the best they could to find moments of joy in their work, in their customers, and in each other.

9

Despite her love for Emma's home, school was a refuge for Mariah. She loved her classes. She loved her violin. She loved her friends, especially Madison, with whom she could share secrets and gossip. But in many ways, Mariah was an adult even at her young age. She cared about her teachers, Ms. Bennington most of all.

The two had grown close throughout the school year. Sometimes, Mariah would take her lunch to her classroom, where Ms. Bennington ate alone at her desk. Mariah asked her questions—many questions, probably too many questions—but Ms. Bennington was always open and honest. She answered the questions she could, even when they were a little too personal.

"Are you married?" Mariah asked her point blank one day.

Taken aback, Miss Bennington formulated her response. "Well, Mariah, I was married. You could say my husband, Thomas, and I grew apart. We didn't . . . we didn't always agree. When we were younger and first married, those years were the best. We traveled a lot, even though we didn't have much money. We ate simply. We saw museums and went to concerts. Our picnics together were my favorite times. In fact, you could say we lived like gypsies."

"Wow, that sounds great," Mariah told her. "Why did you stop all that and grow apart?"

"It's kind of complicated."

"I'm sorry if I'm bringing back bad memories," Mariah said.

"No, not at all. Thomas and I had some very good—no, make that great—times. But then we had Nicole, and Thomas had to get extra work. Well, I did too, and it seemed we were always working, only meeting each other in passing. Our hours weren't the same, and Nicole needed lots of attention, like all babies do. Thomas tried to be a good father—I know that, and I love him for that—but after a while, I guess, it just became too much."

Ms. Bennington looked away, seemingly lost in thought. "I think being a father just wasn't what he thought it would be or could be. Oh, he was always the best dad and loved Nicole until . . . until Nicole got sick. I think it just became too much of a burden for him."

"Your daughter was sick?"

"She is sick," her teacher replied. "She is very sick still, and it worries me to death. I have insurance, but doctors say Nicole needs special care and more specialists. That is, if I can find one and if I can afford one, or more. It worries me, but we get by. Thomas fell in love with another woman, and we divorced. He moved away. We still maintain contact, but it's not much and not often. Nicole and I are pretty much on our own. She's four now and the love of my life, but her health isn't good. Anyway, I don't like to dwell on it or talk about it too much, but . . ."

Mariah smiled at Ms. Bennington. "You know, I'd like to be like you one day. I think I'd like to be a teacher, especially an English teacher."

Ms. Bennington let out a small laugh. "That's a good thought, and you're very good in English, but explore all your options. You're young, and life holds endless possibilities. Now, we both better gobble what's left of our lunches and get ready for class. You have math next, right?"

"Yes," Mariah said. She finished her sandwich and wrapped a cookie Helen had made her in a napkin before putting it in her pocket.

"If I know Barbara Randolph, Mrs. Randolph, you better scoot so you can get in your seat early. And you better be ready to listen. So off you go, but Mariah . . . know how much I appreciate you. We will talk more another time."

Mariah did as she was told, but she kept thinking about Ms. Bennington into the night. In bed, she thought about how sad the divorce must have been. Most of all, she wondered about Nicole and what illness she had. It sounded bad.

After a fitful night of sleep, Bella awakened Mariah by gently licking her face. The dog wanted more than a snuggle, though. She seemed intent on telling Mariah something. Even before showering and dressing for the day, Mariah knew it was important to pay attention.

From their first meeting, she had understood Bella's natural abilities to communicate, and she knew it was important to look, listen and learn. She sat on the floor next to Bella and returned Bella's gaze. Bella took her time, sending messages in fragments and images. Mariah looked deeply into Bella's eyes and saw an image of a young woman, like a snapshot or photograph. The girl appeared to be about nineteen or twenty, with long auburn hair, very fair skin, and a shyness that Mariah could almost feel. The girl also had very big ears, too big for her fragile face. They seemed to protrude out like headphones. It wasn't that the ears were repulsive or freakish; it was more that the ears stood out because the girl was self-conscious. As a result, they seemed to take prominence over her beautiful face and glowing chestnut eyes.

She was pretty, whoever this girl was, but she wore a look of loneliness. Her shame stopped her from projecting the true beauty she was inside and out. Bella said the girl often came to the bakery right after Mariah left for school; they missed each other by just a few minutes. Broken phrases and images formed a pattern of the girl sitting alone, nibbling on a croissant, shyly looking around, and then leaving with undisguised sadness.

Bella believed that Mariah and Emma should help her. Mariah stroked Bella's fur.

"I will try," she assured her pet. "But for now, I need to get ready. I can't be late for school. Please be good, keep watch, and be kind to Sasha."

She rushed through a shower and dressing before going to the bakery. Mariah scooped Bella up into her arms and took her to the bakery. Bella loved to watch the world and the customers from her soft bed tucked into one corner. The dog never barked or bothered customers, and the customers often asked Helen or Emma whether they could pet her. But most of all, Bella listened.

It wasn't quite seven that morning when the girl appeared just as the bakery opened. It was earlier than she usually visited, but she was just like Bella described. She quietly ordered her usual croissant and black coffee, then took a seat at one of the small tables. She kept her head down and nibbled away at her breakfast.

Mariah smiled at Helen, then approached the girl. "Hello! Would you like anything else today?"

"No, thank you," the girl replied simply.

Mariah gave her a warm smile. "Thank you for coming to our Kind House Bakery. I'm Mariah, and I work here when I'm not at school most days."

"Nice to meet you, Mariah. My name is Becca."

"Welcome, Becca. We're so glad you're here. Please let us know if we can help in any way." With that, Mariah went back to the kitchen and gathered her things for the bus ride to school. On the way, she noticed Bella watching the girl. The girl looked up, then smiled forlornly back at the dog.

That night, after dinner, Mariah told Emma about her day, as she usually did. It was always a special time for the pair, just the two of them spending time with each other and expressing the love and joy they shared.

Bella rested near Mariah's legs until Mariah started telling Emma about the girl. Bella scooted out from under the table and rose on her hind legs to share in the story.

"Why do you think Bella is so interested in Becca?" Emma asked. "And why do you believe she was so insistent with you?"

Mariah paused. "You know, you're right. Why, of all the customers that come and go, did Bella choose her? And why now?"

"Why, indeed," Emma said with a wink. "There is a reason, dear, and you and I both know it. You have really grown and done so well in school and in helping me here. You're becoming your own person and sharing your soul. I am so proud of you. And, I guess, I don't ask often enough about your thoughts and your world and . . ."

"And the telepathic gifts?" Mariah asked.

"Yes, those," Emma said. "You knew soon enough I would bring that up, didn't you?"

"Yes, I guess I did. I tried the skills you suggested, and I taught myself to use those gifts sparingly to look at the world and people around me. I tried to be aware and, if possible, to seek ways to help others, and . . ."

"And?" Emma encouraged her to go on.

"And I have been seeing." Mariah told Emma about her friend, Madison, and about Ms. Bennington and her sick daughter. Mariah now realized there was something to be explored with Becca, once her dog brought it to her attention.

"Well, I, too, have a customer story to share

with you," Emma said. "But it was Vihaan and Sasha who brought it to me. Vihaan has, as you know, special gifts of insight and perception. For years now, he and Sasha have become close . . . special friends, you might say. Sasha often spends her day on the emporium's miniature Egyptian throne that sits high over the counter in the Emporium and keeps watch over the comings and goings. That beautiful cat watches, listens, and learns, just as Bella does, and as we do sometimes. We probably should do it more often."

Emma sighed sweetly. "We have things— life things, important things—that must take precedence, though."

Mariah nodded with anticipation and a hint of impatience. "Go on."

Emma smiled at her daughter. "So, you think I dawdle or draw out what can be said quicker?"

She laughed, and Mariah chuckled out an apology. "I'm sorry. I didn't mean to be rude."

"Oh, you weren't rude, dear. It's just a fact of life. Young people want results, want immediate action, want to cut to the chase, as the saying goes. Well, here is where Vihaan, Sasha, and I are so similar. We wait to get all the puzzle pieces together before attempting to complete the puzzle. As the years pass, you will see. But back to the present," Emma said, shifting gears.

"It seems a nice young man—twenty or twenty-two, Vihaan guessed—has been coming to the emporium frequently over the past few weeks. Never two days in a row or at the same time of day, but frequently. Vihaan watches as the young man walks up and down the packed rows of books, antiquities, oddities, and rarities. Most often, the man searches the shelves containing potions or charms.

"Can I be of help searching for something?" Vihaan asked, only to be told no.

"I'm just sort of looking for, well, something that would maybe help me with . . ."

"Yes. Yes. Something to help you in business, life, or love?"

"I guess you could say love," the bashful young man said.

"Vihaan would recommend this or that, but nothing really interested the young man," Emma continued. "So, he keeps coming back day after day. It was Sasha who told Vihaan the young man was lonely, shy, and had little experience in relationships aside from a brief girlfriend or two in high school. Sasha saw into his heart and reported through images and purrs what the young man sought and why.

"Now, Mariah, perhaps we can kill two birds with one stone, though I hate that expression. Maybe we better say we can help two people with one objective."

"Love?" Mariah asked dreamily.

"Yes," Emma replied. "Or, at least, an end to loneliness or the beginning of a friendship that could lead to love. Why not? We are here on Earth to serve a purpose, and what greater purpose is there than helping others?"

Mariah clapped her hands. "I agree, and love is a great cause. I hope to find love or fall in love someday."

Emma giggled. "Oh, you do, do you? Well, my young daughter, love will come—romantic love, that is—when it's time and when it's right. And usually, it just happens. But in some cases, it needs a nudge."

"And we can be that nudge?" Mariah asked.

"Yes." Emma replied. "We can nudge, but it's up to those being nudged, so to speak, to make sure it's right."

"Okay, so how and when do we nudge?"

"We'll see," Emma said simply. "We'll see. But, for now, let's listen to some music and wind down from our day. Music hath—"

Mariah finished the sentence for her. "The charms to soothe a savage breast. I know just the right one."

She turned on *Scheherazade* and turned down the lights. The pair settled into their soft chairs. Emma thought through the day's events, and Mariah dreamed about being an exotic princess swirling in fine silk cloth as she danced gracefully to charm a handsome prince.

10

The whole family worked on the game plan. They would create the perfect romantic encounter for their two customers, helping two people with one objective.

To the young man named Philip, Vihaan suggested a vial that held a potion made of musk from a musk ox, cinnamon, willow bark, and strawberry seeds. It was to be worn lightly like a cologne, but very lightly, with just a tad on his neck and forearms.

Emma and Mariah had an idea for Becca. Mariah paraded into the bakery wearing her beret and asked Becca to place her hair just so and try on the hat. That would minimize her ears and reinvigorate her self-confidence.

Mateo, Veronica, and Delores devised a way to have Becca and Philip come to the restaurant on the same day at the same time.

"But how?" Mariah asked. "How could that be arranged without giving away our plan?"

Mateo spoke up first. "Vihaan, you invite Philip to be your guest because he has been a good customer. You work out the day and time to fit with the same day and time that Emma, Mariah, and Helen invite the young woman— Becca, yes?"

Mariah smiled and nodded. "That's a good plan, but, I mean, it's going to be hard to make it work for both."

Emma placed her hand on her daughter's shoulder. "Well, I know you have heard me say this: Where there's a will, there's a way. Plus, we have the power of suggestion. Let's get to work."

And work they did. It took some negotiations back and forth, but both sides suggested, pushed, and prodded. They would not take no for an answer from Philip or Becca. As a cherry on top, Becca loved the beret so much she and Mariah went to the boutique where Mariah bought hers and found the perfect one for Becca.

It was a soft golden crème color that highlighted

her beautiful hair and eyes. Becca loved it so much that she wore it day after day. Their young customer had come to enjoy the friendship with Mariah, treating her like a younger sister and Emma as a second mom in a way.

Vihaan faced more of a challenge. Philip was smart—too smart, perhaps—and he suspected that something was up. But with Vihaan's understated intelligence, the two forged the beginning of a friendship. They both liked ancient history and loved to play chess.

Philip came by the shop when he could, and they played chess, sipped tea, and discussed life. Vihaan discovered that Philip was a lawyer—not in the dramatic courtroom sense, but in a business law way that played perfectly with his keen mind and sharp wit. On top of that, Philip had a good, genuine sense of humor and was an animal lover.

Meanwhile, Emma, Helen, and especially Mariah learned more about Becca. She was an insurance adjustor who had recently moved to a simple-yet-upscale apartment in Brewster. She loved reading, music, horseback riding, and puzzles.

With their background research complete, the

matchmaking team set to work. Mateo planned specific meal specials for the week of the proposed meeting. Veronica and Delores would seat Becca and Philip at neighboring tables along one side of the restaurant that was quiet and softly lit, even at lunch time. Becca would be facing the next table, where Vihaan and Philip would be seated, and Philip would be seated facing Becca.

After they all finished eating, the next step was for Emma to bring Becca to Vihaan's table and introduce him as part of her family and their resident curator of goods perfect for a new apartment. Vihaan would then introduce his friend, Philip.

The moment would come when both tables would be joined together for coffee. Soon after, the family members would trickle out for one reason or another, eventually leaving Becca and Philip alone together.

And they built in a fail-safe: if Becca or Philip tried to leave with the others, Mateo and Veronica could step in and engage them just enough to convince them to stay for a special treat the restaurant had prepared.

The matchmaking group members agreed it

was a fantastic plan. A splendid plan, a workable plan, a complicated plan. "It's like a puzzle," Mariah said.

Vihaan nodded. "Yes, that it is. Like a strategic chess maneuver."

"But," he said in all modesty, "I am a good and experienced chess master. So, we make the first move, no?"

"Yes, and, most of all, remember that life is magic," Emma replied. "Magic *can* happen. And it's not enough most times to just believe in magic. You must be part of the magic itself."

She smiled at each person on the special team. "You are all magic. You all bring such special personalities and gifts, so let's pool our talents, gifts, and resources together and hope against hope that something good and beneficial and yes, *magic* works."

And it did work. What was complicated became natural. After they all made their exits, Becca and Philip remained beside each other, talking naturally and enjoying each other's company. They were so enthralled, in fact, that Mateo had to gently ask them to leave when the café was closing for the day.

Veronica smiled the biggest smile to ever cross her face as she watched Becca and Philip leave the café together, carrying on their conversation. But it was Delores who summed it all up perfectly. "Escoge una persona que te mire como si quiza's fueras magia," she whispered as she leaned her worn elbows on the food counter. *Choose a person who looks at you as if you were magic.*

11

L ife went on, with some days more packed than others. And while most days seemed a bit mundane, other days reflected the magic that can happen if only others pay attention, care, and, above all, act to make things better. It was not enough to simply pray for things to get better or to wish someone well. Emma, Mariah, and Vihaan knew intimately how true that was.

Ms. Bennington was another perfect example. One morning, on her way from the bus to the front of the school, Mariah cut across the teachers' parking lot. She felt drawn to one corner, where she saw her favorite teacher hunched over the steering wheel, sobbing.

Mariah was unsure whether she should approach. She decided to sit under a nearby tree and retrieve her Amulet of Seeing from her backpack. Looking deeply into the stone was like watching a movie of the events causing Ms. Bennington such pain.

Doctor after doctor said that her daughter's case was incurable, that they knew of no treatment that could really even help Nicole. It was so real, so vivid, that Mariah had to put the amulet away and breathe deeply before trying to stand. She did not want to be dizzy as she made her way into her first classroom of the day.

That night, Mariah told Emma all that happened and even showed her the image left on the Amulet of Seeing.

Emma sat quietly for the longest time, until Mariah gently shook Emma's shoulder to get her to look up.

"Yes, dear," Emma said. "Don't get me wrong here. I have deep respect for the medical system and doctors—well, most of them. But like teachers, lawyers, babysitters, and yes, even bakers, some are better than others. Some don't give up so easily. In fact, I know one doctor in particular who fits that mold. I'll call her in the morning."

And Emma did. Sure enough, the highly

respected doctor, an old friend of Emma's from Boston, was happy to help.

"Have the mother contact me," she told Emma. "I'll make the arrangements; money doesn't matter. Her child matters. As you know, I have my own, shall we say, influence and my own ways. Your wonderful husband, Michael, used to say my favorite thing in stubborn or difficult situations: 'It's not over till it's over.' And love is an important factor in healing. It is like magic and can have a profound effect on the healer and the person needing healing. Jesus is a profound example of that, with all his miracles from healing the leper to raising Lazarus from the dead."

The doctor paused and laughed into the phone. "I realize the American Medical Association would probably disagree with me, but that makes it more fun. Have this Ms. Bennington contact me immediately . . . today."

Emma arranged a meeting during Ms. Bennington's off period. All the details were set: The flights, their hotel stay, travel money, time off from the school. And like magic, like a miracle, after two months of treatment Nicole Bennington was symptom-free and pronounced cured. A surgical procedure, along with medication, did the trick.

As Mariah had learned from living with Emma, magic wasn't a rare thing. It was there to be used every day, if you acted.

Despite all the magic around them, the situation with Judith hadn't changed. In fact, it seemed to grow worse by the day. Vihaan looked at Emma with sadness clouding his eyes, but he never said a word about her sister-in-law.

Mateo, kind Mateo, would shake his head and make the Sign of the Cross. "Madre de Dios, keep that Diabla woman from this place," he muttered under his breath. "I'm afraid she has only evil in her heart."

Helen seemed to suffer the most lately. Almost daily, she wiped away tears with her apron after yet another rebuke from Judith. Helen thought about quitting, but she just couldn't. *It would be like leaving my family,* she told herself.

Mariah, strong in spirit and fearful of little, finally approached Judith one day with a simple question. "Why are you so miserable?" she asked. "And why do you make everyone around you so miserable?"

Judith paused and squared her shoulders, standing inches from Mariah's face. "Because, you foundling, the world is tough. And the sooner you learn that—all of you—the better off we'll be. Not everyone is as foolish as my sister-in-law. Life is not a charity or a game. It's hard work, and, most of all, it's sacrifice. It's—"

"Magical," Mariah interrupted, followed by a giant grin. "The world is magical if you allow it to be."

"Rubbish!" Judith exploded. "Magic is a child's game, a fantasy, and life is real."

"I'm sorry you don't see it," Mariah replied. "But I know life is beautiful, or it can be if you let it. If you look for beauty, you will find it. And if you let the magic and wonder of the world into your heart, miracles can and do happen."

"Oh, you foolish child! Have you learned nothing from your early experiences, other than you got lucky in ending up here? Lucky, pure and simple. Magic had nothing to with it. Magic indeed," Judith snorted. "The only magic is that you're not back on the streets, where you probably belong, after all."

Stung by Judith's words, Mariah took a moment for a deep breath before regaining her smile. "Miracles can happen, and, yes, I know it was a miracle when Emma took me in. It was a miracle when Bella came to me. And Judith, I hope a miracle can come and change your heart."

Judith shoved Mariah aside, then stormed out the front door. "You're wasting my time, and I'm in a hurry this morning. A real hurry, and I'll not be held up any longer by child's talk."

She flopped into the driver's seat, slammed her car door, and sped away, leaving a cloud of dust in her wake.

At noon, Emma's cellphone rang with horrible news. Mariah was in class, so she wasn't told until later that afternoon. After school, Emma took her by the hand and led her upstairs before collapsing into one of the oversized easy chairs.

Not crying, but certainly not able to get the words out entirely, Emma spoke up. "It's bad. Oh Mariah, it's terribly bad."

"What's bad, Emma? What's the matter?"

Emma looked at her through sad eyes. "A car wreck," she replied. "A terrible, terrible car wreck, and Judith is hurt badly. She suffered a head injury, which is the main concern. The hospital found my number in her purse and called me. I went down there immediately. They don't know, really. They don't know."

"Don't know what?" Mariah asked gently as she kneeled by Emma and held her hands.

"Whether she will make it. Whether she will live or . . ." Emma couldn't bring herself to say the final word. "The doctor said Judith is in a coma. She is in intensive care and will be for some time. We must all do what we can. Now, please give me some alone time. But you have my permission—no, my instructions—to tell the others about the incident and to promise that as we know more, we will share updates."

Emma was a constant presence at the hospital, and she arranged to cover all of Judith's expenses. She would visit her sister-in-law, who still was in a coma, to make sure she didn't feel abandoned.

Doctors explained that, in an accident like this one, the major concern is how much they can recover or whether there is a need for additional surgery. It was still too early to know. Judith had not sustained any other major injuries: No other broken bones, no neck or spinal injury, and no abnormal vital signs. Until she came out of the coma, not much more could be done, other than to closely and constantly monitor her.

Emma brought Mariah on some of her visits. They sat beside Judith's bed, taking turns offering soothing words of encouragement, holding her hand, and, other times, just receiving updates from the doctors and nurses.

After several days, Emma knew what must be done. Since Judith's head injury was so severe, it was apparent she would not be able to care for herself or keep up her apartment.

Enlisting help from the family, they gathered her belongings. Some went to storage, while Mateo and Vihaan took some to Emma's spare bedroom, should Judith recover enough to be released at some point from the hospital.

It was Mariah who decided Judith needed something tangible with her as a comfort. Patients in the Intensive Care Unit usually don't get to have any belongings there, other than perhaps a few cards. She could not even have flowers. There was talk by the doctors that if she came out of the coma, they would consider moving her to a room where things could be brought in, but that was still uncertain.

Vihaan spoke first. "I think Mrs. Bleary is Catholic, so maybe we should give her some nice rosary beads to hold."

Emma smiled and thanked him. "No, dear Vihaan. For all these years that I have known Judith, she never seemed to be a practicing Catholic, even if that was her background. Good thought, but let's keep thinking."

The voices, the intuitions kept nagging Mariah. They told her something of comfort might help. She was determined to find it, whatever it was. While the others prayed, meditated, and sent healing vibes, Mariah and Vihaan conspired to seek the right talisman, the right gift for Judith.

One Saturday morning, as she helped Vihaan dust and sort items in his shop, Mariah felt a warm sensation from two shelves over. The sensation was like a magnet, pulling her around the emporium. It became a game of sorts as Mariah sought out the source. She would look right, then get the sensation to look left. She would look down, then get the sensation to look up. And so, the game went on.

Mariah giggled as she played the game, getting warmer. No, cold. Warmer. No, colder. She peered here and there and scrutinized the shapes and objects on the shelves. Finally, after what seemed like hours but was really minutes, Mariah looked up and saw a shape that beckoned her. Stretching on her tippy toes, she could almost, but not quite, make it out.

Vihaan, who had been watching her with glee, brought over the rolling ladder. "Here, miss. Try this to reach your object of desire, or tell me and I'll get whatever it is down for you."

"Thank you, Vihaan," she replied, "but if you don't mind, I think I want to discover whatever it is on my own."

Gripping the rails of the rolling ladder as Vihaan steadied it from below, Mariah climbed nearly to the top and reached onto the highest shelf. She grabbed a bundle of fur, and the object fell to the ground. She rushed down, and together they held up the prize.

It was an old, almost ancient-looking teddy bear with glass eyes and a faded pink bow. It was dusty and dirty, but it held an unmistakable charm. The bear wore a smile, and Mariah could not resist hugging it, dirt and all. It was warm and soft, and it felt so reassuring. Mariah knew then that once cleaned up, it would be the right—no, the perfect—gift for Judith.

Emma wasn't convinced. "Oh, honey, I love your thought," she told Mariah. "That is so sweet, but Judith is no child. Judith is as stern and no-nonsense as they come. She would never give something like that a second thought."

"But she could hug it," Mariah protested. "I mean, once it's thoroughly cleaned and all. It might bring some love to her there in that bed."

"Well, I don't know. Dear, the doctors or nurses might not approve."

"I bet they will," Mariah said. "I'll convince them."

Emma gave in. "Okay, but don't be surprised if it's not allowed or if Judith doesn't respond or take to it. Again, as you know, Judith of all people does not believe in frivolous things, such as a child's teddy bear."

"She will. Besides, she can hug it, and everybody, especially when they're sick, needs a good hug. They need to hold and hug something warm and soft and personal."

"We will see. We will see."

12

A few days later, the phone rang early. Glancing at her watch, Emma saw that it was not quite six in the morning when the hospital called. It was the Intensive Care Unit's charge nurse.

"Can you come to the hospital now?" the nurse asked. "There have been some developments with Mrs. Bleary."

"Developments?" Emma cried with alarm. "Did she die? Did she pass?"

"No, no. Sorry, I should have been more direct at the start. It's just the opposite, I am pleased to report. Your sister-in-law is out of the coma, alert, and saying a few words. The doctors wanted you to be notified immediately."

"Thank you," Emma said, letting out a sigh. "I'm on my way."

Emma told Helen and Mariah about the call, and Mariah desperately wanted to be there with Emma for support and, truth be told, out of curiosity. But Emma declined.

"I'm not sure just how fragile Judith is, and we don't want to overwhelm her," Emma replied. "No. Helen, you manage the shop. Mariah, you go on to school as usual. I'll fill everyone in as soon as I can."

Emma was met at the Intensive Care Unit's entrance by the charge nurse and one of the attending doctors.

"I hate to use the word 'miracle,' but this is certainly unusual. I'll say that," the doctor said flatly. After repeating what the charge nurse told Emma on the phone, he walked off to see another patient.

The nurse smiled. "Let me explain. Would you like to sit?" she asked as she gestured toward a chair along the hallway wall.

"Oh, no, thank you," Emma replied. "I'm just fine to continue as we are."

"All right, then," the nurse said and went on. "It was around five-thirty this morning when I was doing my rounds, checking charts and patients.

I peered in on your sister-in-law. Her eyes were open, and she was clutching that teddy bear your daughter brought her. I stood watching as she smiled at it and attempted to speak. When I approached the bed, Mrs. Bleary looked at me and smiled a thin smile. She slowly said the word Chester and then repeated it."

"Chester?" Emma asked.

"I'm not sure of the significance, but the fact that she is alert and speaking is very positive news," the nurse said. "We will know more later today after we look at her latest test results. It may be possible she can be released in a few days."

"May I see her?" Emma asked timidly.

"No, not yet, unfortunately. I suggest we wait until we have all the facts to avoid overstimulating her. Either myself or another staff member will be in contact. I dare to say, Mrs. McCurdy, that your sister-in-law might be out of the woods and on the road to recovery. It will take weeks, months, or maybe longer to determine the extent of the trauma, but there is no more swelling, no hematoma. Her breathing and other functions are normal. Upon release, whenever we do get there, she will need nursing care and assistance until she is cleared to return to normal activities. But, so far, the prognosis appears good."

"Thank you. Thank you," Emma said softly as tears formed in the corners of her eyes.

"One more thing: Mrs. Bleary keeps thanking the nurses and staff. Her words are halting, but her speech will return. Still, she manages to smile and say thanks to all. She appears grateful and happy. She clutches that toy tightly and won't release it unless she absolutely must. It may be that the soft teddy bear brings her comfort and reassurance. She repeats the word Chester over and over. Do you have any idea who that might be or who she is referring to? Past husband, relative, friend?"

"No, none of those. I have no idea," Emma said. "She actually said thank you? And she smiles?"

"Yes," the nurse said. "It' s always a pleasure to have patients who appreciate us. It's a very positive sign."

"Positive indeed," Emma muttered. "Positive and miraculous."

"Miracles are magic," Mariah told Emma after being filled in on the hospital visit. "That's what you always say."

"Yes, magic is a miracle, but the real miracle is the change in Judith's personality," Emma said. "I told the nurse that Judith's temperament and personality were unpleasant to the highest degree and that she had been mean and horrible to everyone she met. I told them about her negativity in everything she did. The nurse explained that, in some cases, a head injury such as Judith's can actually change their personality. She said it is for the worse, in most cases, not the better. The injury generally makes the person more moody, with outbursts of anger and a negative personality disorder that stays with them the rest of their lives. In Judith's case, it seems just the opposite. She has reverted to almost a child's level of positivity and peace. They said the teddy bear may have triggered some memory she connects with, and that memory may have brought about a change in temperament."

"So," Mariah broke in, "is this change permanent or temporary? Will she go back to her mean self?"

"The doctors could not say for certain. Only time will tell, but I think if we all keep encouraging this new Judith, that maybe, just maybe, it will stick."

"Let's hope so," Mariah added with a smile.

"You know, Mariah, it sounds like your gift may have been the best medicine yet."

Mariah flashed back to that framed picture of Judith as a child, clutching something in shadowy light. "That's it, Emma!" she shouted. "It must be."

"What must be, dear?"

"The photo I saw in Judith's apartment, with some kind of toy! And Chester, the name Judith says over and over again, must have been what she called the teddy bear."

"You must be exactly right, my smart Mariah. Of course! And this teddy bear you and Vihaan found in the shop must resemble the original."

Mariah clapped her hands together in delight. "Or maybe it is the original Chester teddy bear Judith had to give up so many years ago. Vihaan could not recall when or how it came into the shop. He told me it had been there as long as he had been working for you and your husband. Could it . . . could it actually maybe for real be

Judith's teddy bear come back to her?"

"Who knows?" Emma smiled. "Who knows? But it doesn't really matter. To her, it is her Chester. And to us, it is her Chester. The mind and the heart make the magic—always remember that."

"The mind and the heart make the magic," Mariah repeated.

"Now, please gather the others up here. We need to coordinate Judith's care for when she is released. We need a plan of action for meals, care, therapy, transportation, and the like. It will take time for Judith to fully regain her strength. We've already outfitted the spare bedroom with her belongings and an old hospital bed I had in the basement. I will devote myself to her care, but I know we will need a trained nurse periodically. There is much to do here, but with all of us pitching in, we can make it happen."

And happen it did. Day in and day out, night after night, Emma and Mariah were there to give Judith the attention she needed. Judith responded well, so well and so quickly that her health care team was amazed. Soon enough, Judith was up and walking, cheerfully talking with those around her and wanting to help in the daily doings of the businesses.

It was not long before Judith was back at the bakery, but this time she was there to help. To Helen's and everyone else's surprise, Judith was a good worker and a good learner. She asked intelligent questions and applied what she was taught by Helen and Emma.

But, most of all, this new Judith was happy, kind, and, well, a new and completely different person. She whistled cheerful tunes while she worked, and she smiled at and greeted customers warmly. Judith even displayed a remarkable memory for customers' birthdays and the names of their children and spouses.

It did not stop there. Judith informed Emma that she didn't have the funds to repay her for her care and that she didn't have insurance to cover the costs, either. She was eager to work and apply her Emerald Enterprises wages to offset those expenses.

Emma smiled in return and held up her hand to pause her sister-in-law. "Judith, your recovery is enough, and your new personality is worth millions."

"New personality?" Judith asked, surprised.

"Whatever do you mean, new personality? I'm the same as I've always been, aren't I?"

No one replied. Emma just embraced Judith.

And as the months went by, Judith grew stronger and genuinely more interested in the people and happenings around her. She let Mariah help her with makeup and clothing choices, now opting for newer, more colorful styles. The girl also introduced her to all types of music, which delighted the two of them.

In turn, Judith helped Mariah with her schoolwork, especially math and applying it to accounts payable and receivable for the bakery. Judith seemed to have a natural talent when it came to money.

Judith helped the rest of the family, too. On Saturdays, Judith helped Vihaan at the emporium. She complimented him constantly on his impeccable manners and intelligence. Vihaan was stunned, but embraced the new Judith, introducing her to exotic teas, books, and other items from various cultures. In time, they became friends.

Judith dived into learning about Café Esperanza and readily performed any assignment and duty needed, from dishwasher to server and cashier to hostess, under the direction of Delores and Veronica. She always had a smile on her face and an interest in those she served. Judith loved Veronica and treated her like a daughter in some ways. Judith bought little gifts for Veronica, and Veronica taught Judith some Spanish phrases and songs. The two hummed or sometimes sang together after closing, with Mateo accompanying them on his guitar.

Most of all, Judith's change brought a closeness, a bond, between her and Bella and Sasha. She hugged them, sang to them, fed them, cuddled them on her bed, and often took them for walks in the evenings. Each wore a custom leash Judith had ordered from a catalog.

Sasha preened and smiled at the new beaded color Judith gave her, and Bella bounced with joy when Judith would play tug with one of the many new toys scattered around their home. It was the walks in the park, though, that all three enjoyed the most.

Judith lost her disdain for children. Many times, children would approach her to see Sasha and Bella. She would patiently stop and allow the children to pet and talk to the animals. Children seemed to both delight and fascinate Judith, so much so that she began collecting children's books and spending time at the local library.

She learned about books for different ages and watched once a month as the library hosted reading days for young children. Judith delighted in the animated way the librarians read the stories. She watched and learned how the reader made the story come to life, holding up the pages and pointing to the book's colorful illustrations while the children followed along.

It wasn't long until Judith asked Emma about starting a children's reading circle. She and the rest of the family loved the idea. Together, they created Aunt Judith's Reading Room, a small carpeted area with children's furniture in Vihaan's shop. Aunt Judith's readings and free library quickly became a hit, so they added another to one side of the bakery.

What was once the scene of the old Judith's destructive habits gave way to the new Judith's heart of giving. She called it Kind House Children's Hour. The most requested story was one Judith created. Veronica illustrated it with beautiful watercolor images of Bella and Sasha, Emma, Helen, Mateo, Delores, Veronica,

Vihaan, and Mariah, the featured star.

Judith's eyes shined and her voice became musical as she told of how a young, frightened Mariah had left an unhappy situation in search of a better one. One day, the brave Mariah met a new friend, a magical dog named Bella.

Judith went on, detailing the twists and turns of Mariah's magical, mystical, and meaningful adventures. The children always anticipated the close of the story.

"And they all lived," Judith read, then paused. On cue, the children would jump in as a chorus, "Happily ever after!"

King Hill is a well-known and widely acclaimed novelist, historian, award-winning playwright, and stage director. He has lived and continues to live many adventures with passion and purpose. He lives on the High Plains of Texas with his wife in their home warmed with art, antiques, and memorabilia from his theatrical productions and travel.